W9-DAB-903

The Players and the Game

Books by Julian Symons

FICTION

The Players and the Game
The Man Who Lost His Wife
The Man Whose Dreams Came True
The Man Who Killed Himself
The Belting Inheritance
The End of Solomon Grundy
The Plain Man
The Progress of a Crime
The Pipe Dream
The Color of Murder
Bogue's Fortune
The Narrowing Circle
The Broken Penny
The Thirty-first of February
Bland Beginning

NONFICTION

Mortal Consequences

The Players
and the Game

━━ ━━ ━━ ━━ ━━ ━━ ━━ ━━ ━━ ━━ ━━ ━━ ━━ ━━ ━━ ━━

JULIAN SYMONS

HARPER & ROW, PUBLISHERS
New York, Evanston, San Francisco, London

A JOAN KAHN–HARPER NOVEL OF SUSPENSE

FIRST U.S. EDITION

STANDARD BOOK NUMBER: 06–014186–7

LIBRARY OF CONGRESS CATALOG CARD NUMBER: 72-661

Note

This story has similarities to some of the cases mentioned in the text, in particular the Moors Murders and the American Lonely Heart murders. The similarities are deliberate, but they extend only to details. The book is not a documentary, and no theory about any actual murder case should be read into what is emphatically a work of fiction.

J. S.

I

Start of a Journal

Count Dracula meets Bonnie Parker. What will they do together? The vampire you'd hate to love, sinister and debonair, sinks those eyeteeth into Bonnie's succulent throat. The Strangest Couple Ever to Star Together bring to your screens the Weirdest Story of the Century.

That's a heading you'll never see. And it's not the way I meant to start this journal. Excitement got the better of me.

I want to put it down coherently. Of course Bonnie is not Bonnie Parker any more than I'm Dracula, that's part of the Game. The point is that I've never met anybody before who could play the Game, or even understand what it meant. There was a TV program once where they interviewed people coming out after seeing horror films, and asked why they liked them. Some people made a joke of it, nobody answered honestly, but then one chap said, "I like it when the monster gets the girl." That's me, I thought, that's me. I like it too. But I've never met anybody else who would admit that. People are so cowardly. Who do they think they're kidding? Answer: Themselves.

"Thirty Years of Horror Films"—that was the exhibition's title. You can imagine it drew me. And it wasn't a disappointment, even though it was just a lot of stills in an art gallery. But what stills! Bela Lugosi in *Dracula*, cloaked and spotlighted against a wall, and then in *Murders in the Rue Morgue*, one of my favorites. Bela kidnaps women in that one, and then experiments on them with the help of a gorilla. It's all to prove some theory of evolution, but you don't have to worry about that. Lots of other things too. Some modern stuff, almost all rubbish, but there were Chaney and Karloff, a good still from *Frankenstein* with a girl who'd fainted, and *Dracula's Daughter*. I didn't like that much. They were all women. I thought she should have gone for men.

Anyway, I was looking at the *Frankenstein* still when I realized someone was standing next to me. It was Bonnie. She was staring intensely at the girl, I think it was Mae Clarke, lying head down on a bed, helpless. I hardly ever speak to girls, but there was something—what? receptive, I suppose you might say—about her. I said something about it being a good still. She just nodded, but a couple of minutes later we were together in front of another picture. I asked if she liked horror films.

"They're all right. Some of them, some are just silly. I thought there'd be something from *Bonnie and Clyde*."

"That's a Western."

"Yes, but I thought, you know, that shooting scene. All the blood." She looked at me sideways, and I thought: This is someone I can talk to. So I did. We went out and had coffee, and I talked while she listened. Mostly about my Theory of Behavior as Games. I'd never talked properly to anybody about it before.

The idea about the Theory of Behavior is that we all imitate somebody, but very few of us admit it. In the early sixties, for instance, lots of the young were imitating the Beatles—dress, long hair and so on—but mostly they didn't know that. We all think we're original, though we're really copies. Everybody pretends. Clerks imagine they're famous footballers, or pretend they are managing director, sometimes both. Of course it's all a fantasy; there aren't many famous footballers, and for every managing director there are a hundred or a thousand people who have to take orders. We're all playing games. The point is, you get more fun out of life if you admit this. You can let your fantasy run free, and that's exciting.

I hope this makes sense. It does to me, but at the moment I'm writing in a state of what you might call euphoria. Anyway, at this point I took a risk. I leaned over the table and said, "Do you know who I am? I'm Bela Lugosi."

She just stared at me, and my heart sank. I thought she regarded me as just a nut. But I went on. "And you know who you are? Faye Dunaway."

She shook her head and said, "I'm not." I was ready to get up and go. But she was inspired. "I'm Bonnie Parker."

"And me?"

"You're Dracula."

And of course she was absolutely right. Dracula and Bonnie are much more exciting than Bela and Faye. And this book is to be about Dracula and Bonnie, just them. Nothing else. I've not put anything down here for a couple of weeks, because I wanted to get my feelings straight before writing anything else.

I think I've got it clear now. What it comes to is that Count Dracula and Bonnie Parker together pack a real explosive force of fantasy, games fantasy. Already I've said things to Bonnie that I've never said to anybody. Or Dracula said them to her. I told her about the excitement of that first moment when the sharp teeth sink in. The first pinprick. Then the color of blood, real ruby red. The sight of it running in a slow stream. And Bonnie understood; it was something we shared. That's never happened before, not to Dracula. He and Bonnie shared something.

Whoa. Time to call a halt.

Let me make it clear. Dracula understands it; Bonnie does too. There has not been, will not be, any question of sex between them. Dracula's played a different game, a sex game, with other people, but here sex just does not come into it. You could go further. I don't come into it, or if I do it's only as referee in the Game. What does the referee do but blow his whistle when the rules have been infringed? It's Dracula and Bonnie who play the Game, and they know they're only playing. How can they be anything else, when their reality doesn't exist outside the screen, outside their conversations? Nothing they think or say counts. In their imaginary reality they have a perfect relationship.

I'm very euphoric.

2

Buying a House

━━ ━━ ━━ ━━ ━━ ━━ ━━ ━━ ━━ ━━ ━━ ━━ ━━ ━━ ━━ ━━ ━━ ━━ ━━ ━━

"The lounge." Mr. Darling, the estate agent, dipped his head a little, reverentially. The bald spot in the center of his carefully brushed hair showed. The four of them looked at an empty room.

"Terrific." Paul Vane strode toward the French window, opened it, stood gulping in air as though his life depended on it.

Mr. Darling played a trump card. "Beyond the garden the grammar school playing fields. No prospect of building there." He was a smallish man of about forty, neat and precise, one of the smoothly agreeable rather than the barkingly aggressive kind of estate agent.

"A nice room," Alice said without conviction. She looked toward her daughter. Jennifer shrugged.

"It's like any other suburban house. If that's what you want."

Paul did not say to his stepdaughter that Rawley was a town, not a suburb. They went on looking at the house. Alice concentrated on practical details—fitting in her furniture, carpets, curtains, clothing it with character. Paul praised the quietness of the road, and said how marvelously solid these Edwardian houses were. Mr. Darling prattled on about the convenience of shops and schools (foolish, Alice thought, when Jennifer was

5

obviously too old for school), about tradesmen who delivered. When she murmured that they would think about it, he made it clear that with a house like this, in a road as desirable as this one, they shouldn't think too long.

In company the Vanes were, as other people said, a couple who obviously got on well. You could hardly imagine them quarreling. It was true that they never quarreled, but this was because when they were alone they avoided any delicate or controversial subject. That night, after they had returned to London and Jennifer had gone off, as she blankly said, to meet somebody, they talked in their Chalk Farm maisonette about the Rawley house. The conversation was up to a point typically evasive.

"I can't imagine why you said we'd think about it instead of settling straightaway." Paul flung himself to the floor rather than sat on it, put his head against her legs, grinned with conscious boyishness. "What's up, honey—did you hate the house?"

"It's an ordinary house. I suppose it could be nice."

"You'd make it perfect. You've got the touch."

"It will take you longer to get to work. Jennifer too." The offices of Timbals Plastics, in which Paul was personnel director, were in Westminster. Jennifer had a secretarial job in Mayfair with some film distributors. "She's made it plain enough that she doesn't like it."

"She'll fly the coop any day now, get a flat of her own."

"I wish I knew who the friends are she goes out to meet. Why doesn't she bring them back here?"

"Because the young are young and we're middle-aged, and never the twain shall meet. Not that anyone would ever think *you* were forty-two." She knew that Paul wanted her to say that he looked thirty-five instead of forty, but she refused to coddle his vanity like that. Anyway, it wasn't true any more. He had kept his figure, but his hair was thinning and his face was lined. He had been wonderfully handsome, and she had always loved handsome men. She regarded herself as a practical woman, and

6

her liking for masculine good looks as a sentimental weakness, but it still remained. Her first husband, Anthony, had looked like Rupert Brooke. He was ten years older than she, an air force pilot whose plane had crashed in the Alps when she was eight months pregnant with Jennifer. As for Paul, he now looked what he was, a man of forty. Did you call somebody of that age handsome any more? "Here it's a fairly crummy maisonette, there you've got green fields. So what's against it?"

"I don't see why we have to live in Rawley at all."

"We've been into that." He got up and started to walk about. He could never be still for long. "Look, the chief factory's at Rawley, half the executives live there, Bob Lowson is there—"

"So you have to live there too?"

"Oh my God." He smacked his forehead in mock despair. "You know Bob said he couldn't imagine why we stayed in London, how good it would be to have us as neighbors."

"And what Bob Lowson says you do?"

"It's not like that. You're being unfair, honey."

She knew that she was being unfair. Bob Lowson was the managing director, and his words were meant as an act of friendship. Paul looked at her with the wounded-little-boy stare that had once melted her heart. Now it seemed to her an irritating affectation. She abandoned Lowson, and spoke out of this irritation.

"I just don't want anything to happen again."

"I don't know what you mean."

"Like Monica."

"That was ages ago. You're not holding that against me."

"I don't hold anything against you. I just have a feeling about Rawley. It looks a pretty ghastly place to me. And I think it's bad luck for us."

"It isn't like you to talk about luck."

"I tell you, Paul, if anything else happened like Monica I should leave you."

She hardly ever said such things, partly because they broke

the unspoken rule that they were not people who let their feelings show, and partly because she knew the extravagance of Paul's reactions, but still she was not prepared for him to go down on his knees and weep, and swear that if she left him he would kill himself. Mixed up with this there were promises, and some stuff she did not understand about people gunning for him in the office. After ten minutes of this she agreed that tomorrow he would pay a deposit on Bay Trees, which was the name of the house.

Afterward, lying awake in her separate bed, she said the address to herself silently: Bay Trees, Kingsnorton Avenue, Rawley. It occurred to her that he had got what he wanted, and she wondered why she had opposed going to Rawley so strongly. It was sensible to keep in with the managing director, and what did it matter where you lived, after all?

It was two months since they had tried unsuccessfully to make love, and now, between waking and sleeping, she imagined a man of twenty-five in bed with her, dark, eager, intense. He whispered words that she strained to hear, and she murmured something back to him. Paul moved in his sleep, and groaned.

3

The Lowsons

━━ ━━ ━━ ━━ ━━ ━━ ━━ ━━ ━━ ━━ ━━ ━━ ━━ ━━ ━━ ━━

Bob Lowson pressed a button set in what looked like a decorative wall panel. The panel moved upward and the drinks tray inside came out. He watched the operation with pleasure, poured two large whiskies, gave one to Valerie, and said, "What do you mean, something funny?"

"Don't ask me, I don't know. Just there's something funny about him, that's all."

"Paul gets on with people. I mean, it's his job. So why don't you want him to live here? It's convenient in every way; he ought to be near the Rawley operation."

"All right."

"Anyway, how could I stop him?"

"You didn't have to encourage him."

"It's settled now; they've paid a deposit."

They were two big handsome people. She was only three or four inches below his six foot one. Lowson, a northern boy who had come south and made good like many others, somehow resembled a pig in spite of his fine straight nose and the elegant wings of graying hair that he had blow-waved every month. Valerie, ten years his junior, was a pink rose with blond hair and an hourglass figure. About her flourishing opulent attraction there was something piglike too.

9

"We ought to have them to dinner, introduce them to some people."

"You think they'll fit in?" She shook her head when he laughed. "It's not a joke. I'll bet she's got some funny ideas. I shouldn't be surprised if she was a vegetarian." Valerie was rarely happier than when cutting into a steak. "There's something funny about them *both.*"

He made a characteristic sound, a blend of mannish laugh and piggish snort. "Just ask them to dinner in the next couple of weeks; they'll be all right. Where's Sal?"

"Tennis club."

His nod said that the tennis club was a good place to be. Bob Lowson was the chairman. He was also president of Rawley Cricket Club, and a vice president of the amateur dramatic society and of an ex-servicemen's group. He liked to be involved in local activities.

Like her father and mother, Sally Lowson was big, without being inelegant. Partnering the club secretary, Peter Ponsonby, against Ray Gordon and Louise Allbright, she loped about the court hitting baseline forehands, reaching what looked like winners and returning them, getting up athletically to smash. When they had won the set six–four, Peter embraced her. "You were wonderful. I think that calls for a long cooling drink all round." In the bar he said, "Ray wasn't pleased, not pleased at all. It won't do that young man any harm to be taken down a peg." In the same breath and without any change of tone he went on, "Ray, what are you having? I was just saying to Sally that she played a wonderful game."

Ray Gordon was in his mid-twenties and had played for the county. He was a small neat man, a journalist on the local paper. He said amiably enough that Sally's shots had been going in. When Louise Allbright came out of the dressing room Ray took her by the arm and said that he would take a rain check on that drink if Peter didn't mind. Sally dropped one eyelid in a wink.

Then Ray and Louise went out together, and the zoom of his Triumph Spitfire could be heard.

"Somebody is getting too big for his boots." Peter had the round face of a cherub, scored by two lines of disappointment from nose to chin. He was a bachelor in his forties, and was thought by some members to be queer. His conversation was either amusing or boringly gossipy, according to your taste. "And I've heard of cradle snatching, but really. She can't be much more than eighteen. And I thought you and Ray—"

"You shouldn't think so hard, Peter dear; it's bad for you." Sally went off to the changing room. Standing under the shower, feeling the water hot and hotter and then deliciously cold, she thought that she was pretty bored with the tennis club and with the whole Rawley scene. She was bored with tinpot little journalists like Ray Gordon. Making love in the back of a car had ceased to be exciting, and she was too big a girl to find it comfortable. Louise, now, would be a much better fit. She puffed powder at her body and said aloud, "I wonder if he's laid her yet." Then she went home and there, passionately hungry, devoured a leg of chicken from the refrigerator.

4

Meeting People

━━ ━━ ━━ ━━ ━━ ━━ ━━ ━━ ━━ ━━ ━━ ━━ ━━ ━━ ━━ ━

In early May the Vanes were invited to dinner by the Lowsons. They had not yet completed the purchase of Bay Trees. A query raised by Paul's solicitor had remained unanswered for a couple of weeks. Then it had been cleared up, and everything seemed so straightforward that Paul and Alice had moved some of their furniture out of storage into the empty house. In buying and selling a house, however, nothing is finally settled until the contract has been signed by both parties; and now the solicitors for the seller, a man named Makepeace, had told Paul through Mr. Darling that they had received a higher offer.

On the way to the Lowsons', Paul and Alice called on the estate agent. His office was in the old part of town, in an eighteenth-century house with an elegant bow window. Paul had worked himself up into a state of anger that was part synthetic and part real.

"I'm bound to say that to do what your client has done—accept an offer, let us pay a deposit and then look for a higher offer behind our backs—seems to me pretty outrageous."

Mr. Darling, head bowed and tonsure showing, heard this assault with composure. "I should go further." His voice was low but audible. "I should say it shows bad faith. Which is something I am not prepared to tolerate."

"We took it that he was honest, and we've moved some stuff in already. If the whole deal's off I shall expect compensation." Paul paused. "What's that you said?"

"I put this to Mr. Makepeace, and said that I could no longer act on his behalf if he considered another offer after accepting yours."

"That's all very well, but—" Paul paused again, considering the small firm jaw that faced him across the table.

"I am happy to say I have been able to get Mr. Makepeace to agree. He did have a higher offer—not made through me, I can assure you—and he was tempted. I don't think he quite understood the ethics of the situation. I told him that he was bound in honor not to consider any other offer."

"And?" It was almost the first word Alice had spoken at the interview.

"And he has turned down the other offer." He pressed a buzzer. A flabby-looking woman with mouse-colored hair came in. "Miss Brown, the letter from Mr. Makepeace's solicitors, please. And the carbon of my acknowledgment."

Miss Brown brought them in. The solicitors' letter confirmed that they were going ahead and would be ready to exchange contracts within a couple of days.

"You'll no doubt be hearing from your own solicitors. Our postal services are not what they used to be." He smiled shyly at this, then grew serious. "You'll have a beautiful home, Mrs. Vane. In the best part of Rawley."

"The best part of Rawley," Alice repeated as they got out of the car and she looked at the red brick Edwardian houses around them, each with its separate garage and well-kept front and back gardens. They went around the empty house again, looking for cracks in ceilings, sniffing in the damp cellar. "Are you having second thoughts? It's not too late."

"No second thoughts. I told you, it's going to be terrific."

"I hope I can take life in the best part of Rawley, that's all."

"You know the finest cure for crime? Health." Sir Felton

13

Dicksee looked challengingly around the table. He was chief constable of the county, and nobody cared to contradict him. The men were still in the dining room after dinner, on their second glass of port.

"You mean the criminal type is mentally abnormal?" Dick Service, keen and doggish, was the Timbals Plastics psychologist.

"Not mental. Let you trick cyclist chaps get going and you tell us we're all abnormal, more or less." Sir Felton laughed heartily. "May be right for all I know, but it's not what I'm talking about. Talking about health, keeping fit. No need to spend too much time on it. Ten minutes a day with the Dicksee diaphragm exercises will keep you in trim." He slapped his solar plexus, which reverberated like a drum, then got out of his chair, touched his toes and kicked up each leg high as a ballet dancer.

"Splendid," Dick Service said. "But do you mean that if all crooks did this they'd become honest citizens?"

Sir Felton snorted. He was a small red peppery man with a thick mustache. "Course not. I'm not a crank. What causes crime? Bad housing, wrong food, environment generally, right?"

"It certainly has a lot to do with it," Dick Service agreed diplomatically.

"Right. Bring up people in healthy conditions, give 'em light, air, make 'em take exercise whether they want to or not, and you'd cut the crime rate by a quarter in ten years."

"What about heredity?" Paul Vane asked. Sir Felton made a derisive noise. "And then what about the exceptional criminal?"

"Never met one. Have you?" The chief constable drained his glass, glared across the table. "They don't exist. Believe me, I know."

"Just people who don't do the Dicksee diaphragm exercises." The words came out with an ironic effect that was not intended.

There was silence. Then Bob Lowson smoothly led the conversation to golf handicaps, and went on to suggest that Paul should think about joining Rawley Golf Club. When he admitted that he did not play there was again a moment of silence.

In the drawing room the ladies talked about the latest films, and in particular about *Little Woman, Big Man,* which had been showing at the Odeon. Too much sex, Lady Dicksee said decisively. Why couldn't they realize that people went to the cinema for entertainment?

In her breathless apologetic voice Penelope Service disagreed. "I mean, it was all rather, didn't you think, sweet? Especially this girl, you know, the one who was almost, well, raped on board the boat."

"Karen Vallance," Valerie contributed helpfully.

"I thought Karen Vallance was the one in the dress shop."

"That was Marianne Musgrave."

"No, Marianne Musgrave was the one thumbing a lift, the one who said, 'I'm Satan's daughter.' "

They appealed to Alice, but she had not seen the film. She did little better when the talk turned to education and she said she thought university was not important for most girls and that she was quite pleased Jennifer was in a job. It turned out that Sally Lowson had just come down after taking a second—but a very good second—in social science, and was now a managerial trainee at Timbals, and that the Dicksees' son and daughter had both got splendid jobs for which a university degree was an essential qualification. When the conversation moved to gardens Alice was silent. They had had no garden in Chalk Farm. She stayed silent when they went on to the running of a jumble sale for Oxfam, for which Valerie Lowson was acting secretary.

When they had all gone Valerie and Bob cleared up. The help came in the morning, so that there was really no need to do this, but the operation of the kitchen machinery delighted them both. The outsize dishwasher got to work on plates and sauce-pans, the waste destructor crunched up rubbish, unused things were hung on hooks.

"You see what I mean," Valerie said. "What's her name, Al-ice, was really a dead loss. The thing is, she doesn't *try* to show any interest."

"Give them a chance; they'll settle down."

"I bet he was no better."

"He put up a black with old Felton. Still, Felton can be a bore."

"I just don't see why you want them here. Yes, all right, I know it's convenient, but I tell you, Bob, you'll be sorry."

When she had that high color Val always seemed to him desirable. He put aside his dishcloth, placed both arms around her, kissed her ear.

"Robert Lowson. At your age."

"That's not so old. Let's go upstairs and play games."

"Where's Sally?"

"Out. Stop worrying. She's a big girl now."

Both of them would have been surprised by the idea that this was literally true. They simply considered most other people as under normal size.

The Services lived near Bay Trees, in a very similar road. They got back to find Anne Marie, the au pair, dancing franti-cally up and down in an attempt to stop their two-year-old son, John, from screaming. He had stuffed a teddy bear into his mouth until he choked, and had been screaming ever since. It turned out that he was soaking wet. He stopped screaming when Penelope caught hold of him, and fell asleep the instant she put him to bed.

Penelope was inclined to blame Anne Marie, saying that she ought to have been there when John was stuffing the teddy bear into his mouth. Anne Marie wept. Later Penelope said to Dick that the girl was slovenly and thought of nothing but getting up to London, and that they really should get rid of her. Dick stayed silent. He knew that Penelope would have forgotten the idea by the next morning. Anne Marie in tears had looked very pretty and rather exciting.

"Do you know what we talked about?" Alice asked as they got onto the main road. "Bedding plants and natural manure and charities and who was in what at the local cinema. God, that Valerie's a bore."

"And what do you usually talk about?"

"Something a bit more intelligent. I don't usually meet people like that."

He glanced at her for a moment, then back to the road. "There are wheels within wheels. Hartford is trying to get me out."

She repeated the words incredulously. "You're imagining it."

"He's got some girl in as my assistant. A behavioral scientist."

"What's that?"

"Don't ask me. But she's Hartford's importation. I shouldn't be surprised if she reports back to him. So don't talk too much about Valerie Lowson being a bore. Bob likes me."

"I suppose it's a reason for coming here. Keeping in with the boss." They were on a motorway. The stretch in front of them looked endless. "But I can feel trouble ahead. I really can."

He took a hand off the wheel and put it on her knee, totally without sexual implication. In what she thought of as his actor's voice he said, "No trouble. I swear it."

Brian Hartford lay on the floor, looked through his gun sight and fired four shots. Each pellet struck a foot soldier. He completed the move by wheeling his infantry so that they encircled Blaney's depleted right flank. "Got you," he said in the eager biting tone that made his words often sound like a command or an insult. He was a small sandy man with greenish eyes and almost invisible eyebrows.

Blaney considered the situation. Soldiers, red and blue, horse and foot, covered the plastic-tiled floor. There was a village street with a church in it, a woods made from plastic trees, a blue plastic river with a bridge which Blaney's retreating troops had failed to reach in time to blow it up. He nodded. "Trouble is, your gunners have got twenty-twenty vision." Blaney wore thick pebble glasses.

The remark had a flavor of frivolity which Hartford disliked. It implied that good sight was more important than good generalship. "Not at all. You should have drawn back your left sooner to cover the bridge. You simply didn't realize its importance." He relented and offered whisky. After all, he had won. They went into the living room. Hartford talked exclusively about the game they had just finished, and what setup they should try next week. Blaney tried to show enthusiasm. He had begun to play the War Game because it sounded like fun, but continued only because he was the marketing manager of Timbals and Hartford was deputy managing director. He hoped for some profit from the association, but so far its possible nature was not apparent.

When Blaney had gone Hartford went back into the big room and put the soldiers, guns and landscape away carefully in boxes. He lived alone on the top floor of a large Victorian house in Maida Vale which had been turned into service apartments. He looked out for a few moments into the quiet street, and then went to bed. His bedroom was composed of rectangles that confronted each other angularly: the bed, the Danish cupboard and dressing table, a high-backed chair. He carefully hung up jacket and trousers, put shirt and briefs into a laundry bin and shoes on trees, looked with pleasure at the Mondrian lithographs on the walls, and got into bed.

5

Extracts from a Journal

Saw *Eyes Without a Face—Les Yeux Sans Visage* is the proper French title. All about a doctor who takes skin grafts off people to put onto his daughter's disfigured face. Didn't like it, not interesting. Bonnie didn't come, quite right too. These new films are not like the old ones. Though I liked *Psycho*, that was good. The shower cabinet, the blood running away. And there is one called *Peeping Tom*, which sounds as if it should be good.

There is something that doesn't satisfy me about the Game. What do I mean? I'll try to explain. Take this notebook; who am I writing it for? Myself I suppose, perhaps for Bonnie too, though I'm not *especially* anxious that she should read it. Perhaps I'll let her one day. Nobody else. In a way that's right, I don't want them to, because this is my secret. But in another way I want everybody to know about Behavior as Games, I want them to understand there are no limits to fantasy fun. I want to know the kind of fantasy fun they're having too.

Explained all this to Bonnie, that the two of us were very lucky to be able to tell our fantasies. Not sure she understood, in some ways she's stupid. I believe she thought I was asking her to have sex. Rubbish. I've said it before, but now I shall write

it out in capitals. DRACULA DOES NOT WANT TO HAVE
SEX WITH BONNIE. She wouldn't like it if he did. But anyway,
she doesn't attract him.

Seriously, seriously, Bonnie, that would spoil the whole
Game. What Dracula does want is this—to let somebody else
into the Game. Talked to Bonnie about this, and she was doubt-
ful. I believe when I'm not with her she feels quite differently.
She told me she used to go to church every week when she was
small. When she did anything wrong her father beat her while
her mother watched. Asked if the tortures of the martyrs excited her, lent her one or two of my books about the rack, etc.
She liked it while I was telling her, I could see that, but I don't
know what she felt afterward.

Asked her if she's ever tortured an animal, told her about a
cat I'd seen when I was little. Some boys hung it upside down
and shaved off its fur. Did this happen? And if it happened, did
I take part? Don't know, I get confused. But Bonnie didn't
answer, got upset when I asked again if she'd ever done things
to animals. I believe she has.

I have told Bonnie what I believe. The important thing in life
is Power. Most people are stupid, they don't possess Power, not
even in their fantasies. Everything is petty now. I gave her my
test, quoted the great master Nietzsche to her: "Whatever is of
the effeminate type, whatever springeth from the servile type,
and especially the mob-mishmash:—*that* wisheth now to be
master of all human destiny—O disgust! Disgust! Disgust!"

She seemed to be impressed. Bonnie is in awe of me, recog-
nizes her superior. That is right.

A third person in the Game is vital. There is something sacred
about one—"one is one and all alone"—and about a triangle.
Two is not the same. That has been my trouble in the past. What
is the relationship between Sex and Power?

Later. Have made contact with a Third. Very promising,

although I have been careful. I said nothing of Bonnie. I long for the moment when the three of us meet, when we talk to each other as Bonnie and Dracula have done, secure in the freedom of fantasy.

Have bought a tape machine in preparation. What will it record and repeat?

6

The Disappearances

Anne Marie had every evening free, but it was understood that she would let Penelope know in advance if she was to be home later than eleven o'clock. On the night of May 27 she went out at eight o'clock. Penelope noticed, or remembered afterward, that she looked flushed and excited. She said that she would probably not be back until about midnight.

At two in the morning Penelope went to bed. At breakfast-time Anne Marie had not returned. Penelope and Dick talked about whether they should sack her when she came back. On the following day, Sunday, they got in touch with the police.

On the morning of Wednesday, June 1, Mr. Darling visited Rawley police station. He saw Sergeant Saunders, who knew him quite well by sight as one of the town's half-dozen estate agents. Mr. Darling asked rather hesitantly whether they had heard anything about a secretary-typist named Joan Brown who worked for him. She had not come in on Monday morning, and when he went around to her room to inquire if she was ill, it seemed that she had packed her things and left.

"I see, sir. Had you any hint of this? I mean, did she seem fed up with the job, give you any idea she might be going?"

"None whatever. I was quite satisfied with her work." He

made it sound like a testimonial. "It's surprising. And annoying. She was reliable, which is unusual nowadays. If she's coming back I don't want to engage anybody else."

"Been with you long, had she?"

"Not long, no. About three months."

"Any trouble at home as far as you know, anything like that?"

"Home." Mr. Darling, neatly dressed and wearing a spotted bow tie, considered the word. "I don't actually know where her home is; we never discussed it. She just had a room here. I suppose she came from London." He leaned on the counter. "I expect you think I'm fussing about this, Sergeant, but I don't understand why she left without saying a word to me or sending a letter. It seems out of character."

The sergeant, who did think that Mr. Darling was fussing, said that inquiries would be made. The details of the two disappearances made their way onto the desk of Sergeant Plender of Rawley CID. He talked about them to the head of Rawley sub-Division, Detective Inspector Hurley.

It was a hot day, with the threat of thunder in the air. Hurley's office was uncomfortably warm. He was not a man who sought out work. "I don't see what you're on about, Harry."

"Two disappearances, sir, two in four days."

"You can't say this girl Brown's disappeared. From the report she simply upped and went. Took all her gear, didn't she?"

"Yes, but according to Mrs. Ransom—that's her landlady—she was in a fair old state, had been for a couple of days. And she never said she was going; that surprised Mrs. Ransom just like it surprised her employer, Darling."

"The estate agent, isn't it? I know him by sight." Hurley picked his teeth. "What sort of girl was she, one for the bright lights?"

"No, sir. Rather shy and reserved."

"How'd she go—find that out?"

"No. I've inquired at the station and bus depot, but they don't remember. Not that they'd be likely to. We haven't got a picture."

"Anyway, she left under her own steam, not much doubt about that."

"I suppose not. If it weren't for the other case—"

"The au pair girl."

"That's right. Anne Marie Dupont. Worked as au pair for a Mr. and Mrs. Service. I gather she may have been a bit flighty, but nothing serious. She's left her suitcase behind, clothes, shoes, everything."

The inspector looked at the photograph with Plender's report. "Nice bit of stuff. You might say she was flighty and now she's flown." Plender did not laugh. "So she's left her duds behind. It doesn't mean much. Ten to one she's working in a strip club now where she doesn't need 'em. You know what a lot of these au pairs are—on the game only they like to pretend they're amateurs."

"Yes, sir."

"I see you don't think I'm right. Well, all you have to do to convince me is to show some connection between Miss Brown the secretary-typist and Miss Dupont the au pair. You can't do that?"

"Not at present."

"What about their families?"

"The Services have written to Anne Marie's people in France. I gather her mother's dead; she lived with her father and an elder sister. Haven't traced the Brown woman's family so far."

"Right. *At present,* then, we go through the usual motions. And I think you'll find, Harry, that within a week or two one or both of 'em will turn up." Hurley wiped his forehead.

7

Plastics People

■ ▬ ▬ ▬ ▬ ▬ ▬ ▬ ▬ ▬ ▬ ▬ ▬ ▬ ▬ ▬ ▬ ▬

On the first of June the Vanes moved into Bay Trees. A company car called every morning for Bob Lowson and took him up to the office, but Bob worked on papers and dictated letters while he was being driven, and Paul was not offered a place in the car. He and Jennifer drove or walked to Rawley station and took the train. The journey lasted forty minutes, during which Paul read the *Financial Times* and the *Times*, and Jennifer turned the pages of a women's magazine. Alice was left alone in the house. She made curtains, stained floors, opened accounts with local tradesmen. She was asked to a couple of coffee parties, but mistook the time of the first and arrived when people were leaving, and sat through the local gossip at the second without saying more than a dozen words. She disliked gossip. After returning home she thought: I shan't ever go there again.

She spent part of the afternoon of that day looking through a box of old photographs which she found in the pile of stuff stacked in a spare bedroom. She sat cross-legged on the floor with the pictures spread out around her—Jennifer as a baby crawling over the lawn of a flat they had had near Croydon when Paul was working as a salesman, Jennifer as an angel in a school play, Paul and herself at the firm's annual dance just after he had joined Timbals twelve years ago. Sir Geoffrey Pill-ing, managing director before finance became shaky and Bob Lowson was brought in to reorganize, had danced twice with her. He had said to Paul, "I congratulate you, Vane, on having such a beautiful young wife. You make a fine couple."

Beauty, she thought, beauty. The word rang like a bell down the years. As she remembered it that had been the best time of her life, a time when she had recovered from Anthony's death and had been entranced by Paul's good looks, when she herself had been beautiful and perfectly happy. Her parents had disapproved of Paul, who as her mother had put it was far from being out of the top drawer, but Alice had not cared about that. It was a long time, though, since they had made a fine couple. "I am beautiful," she said, and went on muttering it like an incantation until she had reached the bathroom, and the glass there gave her the lie. This pale creature, still with fine bones and delicate features, but with wild graying hair and something strained about the eyes, was certainly not beautiful. She tore up the photograph at the dance into four pieces, wept a little, carefully stuck the pieces together again with a postcard backing. With these concessions made to sentiment, she became again her practical self. She did her face, put on a dress that was rather too smart, and went out shopping.

In the High Street she met Penelope Service, who told her about the puzzle of the missing Anne Marie. "She's really a bit odd," Penelope said to Dick that evening. "Do you know what she said when I told her about Anne Marie? She said"—Penelope gave a giggle sharp as a hiccup—" 'I wonder if my husband's seduced her? He doesn't like me much now, but he's fond of young girls.' "

Dick nodded. As a psychologist he was professionally unsurprised by anything.

"And *then* she said, 'Don't take any notice; I've been having an afternoon in the past. Do you ever do that?' I felt rather . . . sorry for her; she seemed quite . . . ." Penelope's sentence faded into total extinction. "So I asked her back to tea, and she's going to join the . . . bridge club."

26

"Fine. What are we going to do about that damned girl?"

"I don't think I want to have another au pair. They're more trouble than . . ." Another sentence faded.

"I suppose we'd better send her things back to her family."

"I'll do it tomorrow."

"The police seemed pretty sure she was having it off with some fellow in London. She didn't seem to me quite that type, I must say."

Penelope Service had heard enough about Anne Marie. "I don't know, darling, and frankly I don't care. All I know is that she was a rotten au pair, and I'm . . . glad she's gone."

"It would be funny if Vane really had got her tucked away in a love nest somewhere. Rather a dish, isn't he?"

"Not my type. I don't like men his age pretending to be teen-agers. He looks as if he might dye his hair."

The office door said *Paul Vane* in gold lettering, and *Director of Personnel* beneath it in black. The position had at one time been called Personnel Manager, but the word Director was thought to add prestige. It did not carry with it a position on the board, but Paul was entitled to use the washroom and luncheon room which were used also by board members. Such marks of distinction were important. They showed how far he had come since joining the firm as a junior member of the Personnel Department.

A week after the move to Rawley he found a memo on his desk. It said that next week a small luncheon room was to be opened on the top floor for the use of directors, selected senior staff and their guests. The room would be used only when guests of importance were present. Appended below was a list of those entitled to use the new luncheon room, after giving prior notice of the guests who were being entertained. His name was not on it.

He read the list of names a second time. It was headed by the chairman, Sir George Rose, and included all the directors. Apart from these there were two names on it—those of Blaney, the home marketing manager, and O'Rourke, who was concerned with exports. Obviously Paul Vane should have been on it too. The memo came from Hartford's office, and Paul rang his secretary.

The girl who answered said that Miss Popkin was away ill. "I'm her assistant, Joy Lindley." He explained what he wanted. She said, "I'm awfully sorry, Mr. Vane. I'm afraid it was my fault."

"What do you mean?"

"The memo. It was sent to you by mistake. I really don't know how it happened."

"What do you mean, Miss"—for a moment he could not remember her name—"Lindley. I rang to tell you that my name should be put on, that's all."

It was only when she said doubtfully, "Yes, I see," that he realized his name had been left off by intention. He covered up by saying that he would have a word with Mr. Hartford. She sounded relieved as she said that that would perhaps be best.

When he put down the receiver he felt a gust of anger. This was clear confirmation of what he had said to Alice about Hartford gunning for him. Blaney and O'Rourke were departmental heads on his own level, and to leave his name off a list that included theirs was a deliberate insult. Five minutes later he felt composed enough to speak to Hartford.

In the outer office he saw the girl. She was young, with fluffy pale golden hair. She gave him a nervous smile.

"You're Joy Lindley."

"That's right. Mr. Vane, about that memo. It was all my fault."

"Never mind." Below the desktop stretched slimly attractive legs. "How long have you been here?"

"Three months."

"Like it?"

"Oh yes, very much."

"I'm just going in to have a word with Mr. Hartford. Don't worry, Joy, I shan't bring you into it. That's not necessary at all."

28

"Thank you very much."

You've made a friend, Paul, he said to himself as he passed on.

Hartford looked small behind a big desk. A steel and glass inkstand in the shape of a pair of gear wheels stood on it, together with a chromium photograph frame containing the picture of a woman, and a letter opener. It seemed that the letter opener got little use, for the desk was now, as always, almost completely clear of correspondence. Hartford was known to believe that only an inefficient man had a cluttered desk, a disturbing conclusion for somebody like Paul, who always had a pile of papers which could not be dealt with immediately, but equally could not possibly be shut away in a file.

The senior figures at Timbals used first names to each other, but Paul felt uncomfortable in doing so with Hartford. His manner was more boyishly naïve than usual.

"Brian, I understand the new luncheon room is going to be opened next week, is that right?"

"Quite right."

"Fine. I may have a couple of people I'd like to bring along next Thursday. Not sure yet, but I thought I'd check the opening date with you."

Hartford's voice was like the first frost of winter. "I've sent memos to everybody eligible to use the new luncheon room. You've not had one." It was a statement, not a question.

"You mean the room is for the exclusive use of directors."

"I didn't say that."

"Well, then?"

Hartford's tongue came out and briefly touched his lips in what was undoubtedly a gesture of pleasure. "I should have thought the conclusion was obvious."

Paul felt a flush rising in his neck. He kept his voice quiet. "You mean I'm not to use the room."

"The names of those eligible to use it were on the memo."

"It's not confined to directors. Blaney and O'Rourke's names are on it." He stared across the desk. Hartford huddled on the other side, immobile as a lizard. Paul was pleased that his own voice was still quiet. "You're discriminating against me. If it's good for one departmental head it should be good for others. I shan't let this rest, Brian, I shall take it further."

Hartford nodded. In the outer office Joy Lindley looked at him anxiously. He smiled, patted her on the shoulder, went out.

Bob Lowson spent most of the morning in a huddle with the Timbals accountants and the director of a merchant bank. They talked about financial prospects. In the past five years Timbals had diversified their interests, buying up half a dozen small firms and using them as outlets for new plastics products. Everybody agreed that in the long term this was the right thing to do, but in the short term the return on capital was low, and left them possibly vulnerable to a takeover attempt by their American rivals Primal Products. The purpose of the huddle was to assess the group's state of health if such a takeover attempt were made. It seemed to Lowson premature to call in Sir George Rose and Hartford to this meeting, which like many similar discussions turned out to be entirely inconclusive. There were rumors, but it was after all very likely that no takeover attempt would be made by Primal. Nevertheless it was a trying three hours, and after it Lowson turned down the merchant banker's suggestion that they should lunch together. He ordered a rare roast beef sandwich, and made a telephone call on his private line. He felt in need of relaxation.

The street led off Wimpole Street, and the names on the bells were those of doctors. He pressed one that said *Dr. L. Winstanley.* The buzzer sounded and the door opened. He took the lift to the second floor and went in the door that said *Reception.* A nurse in a white uniform confronted him.

"I have an appointment with Dr. Winstanley."

She consulted a book. "She has no appointment at this time."

"But I telephoned half an hour ago."

"I'm sorry. She cannot see anybody."

Lowson whimpered slightly. "Please, nurse."

"Is it really urgent?"

"Yes."

"Very well. Just a moment." She went into another room, returned. "Dr. Winstanley will see you." When Lowson got up she barred the entrance to the inner room. "On your knees." He dropped clumsily to his knees. "Kiss my shoe. Now the other one."

There was a delicious smell of dirt and shoe polish blended. "Pathetic, you're pathetic," the nurse said. She bent down, lifted him by one ear, pushed him into the room so that he stumbled.

Louise Winstanley nodded from behind her desk. Her features were regular and handsome. The corners of her thin mouth were turned down in an expression of permanent disapproval. "Sit down. What is your trouble?"

"Incontinence, doctor."

"Yes, of course. And what has your behavior been like since I saw you last?"

"Bad, I'm afraid. I just can't help myself."

"Then we must try to help you. Stand up." She came around to stand beside him. Her head came up to Lowson's shoulder. "Take your clothes off. I must examine them to see if they are soiled."

He took off his jacket, then gave another whimper. "I don't like to, doctor. Not in front of a woman."

"Hold out your hands." He did so. She took a pair of handcuffs out of a cupboard and fitted them on his wrists. "You are disobedient, stupid and filthy," she said, and smacked each side of his face hard. "I think Agnes had better come in to help me deal with you, don't you?"

"Yes," he whispered. When the nurse appeared in the doorway he thought he would faint with pleasure.

An hour and a half later and twenty pounds poorer, he was back in his office, relaxed and mellow. He contemplated Paul

Vane, and listened to what he was saying, with the amused languor of a well-fed cat. He liked Paul, and thought of grooming him for some position which would involve his joining the board. It was to keep Paul under his eye as much as for the convenience of having him living near to the works that he had mentioned the possibility of moving to Rawley. Looking now at the subdued anxiety of Paul's expression, he wondered whether promotion was after all a good idea.

"This is really Brian's pigeon, you know that. You've spoken to him?"

"Yes. He just said my name wasn't on the list. If Blaney and O'Rourke can use the luncheon room I should be allowed to use it too."

Childish and petty, Lowson thought, and stupid to run to him for protection. It showed a lack of adroitness. There were other ways of handling this kind of thing. He said that he would have a word with Brian. He looked speculatively at Paul's slender figure, thin but longish hair and fashionably colorful tie. Perhaps Val's doubts were right; perhaps he was a bit too much of a good thing.

"How's life in Rawley? Settling down?"

Paul said it was terrific, marvelous to be out of London, with that note of enthusiasm which managed to sound at the same time both sincere and unconvincing. Alice was finding shopping a bit different but, yes, she was enjoying it too.

From the depth of sensual repletion Lowson considered him. There *was* something odd about Paul. What was he like? An actor playing several parts, not quite at home in any of them? "And your daughter, Jean?"

"Stepdaughter actually. Jennifer. I shouldn't be surprised if she spread her wings soon, flew the coop. Youth, you know. She wants London."

"If there's anything Alice would like to know, tell her to ring Val, she'd love to help. Has Alice joined the Townswomen's Guild yet? Val's on the committee."

"I don't think so. She's joined the bridge club."

"Plenty of time. Settle down first."

"As soon as we're straight you must come round and have dinner."

"Plenty of time. Didn't you tell me you played tennis? You should join the club. Sally's a member."

"I'm meaning to. Just for these next few days I'm going to be pretty busy."

"I know. Still you want to join one or two things, keep in the swim."

Paul got up. "You won't forget . . ."

"What? Oh no, leave it to me."

When he was alone Bob Lowson closed his eyes. The day had been exhausting, and he could easily have fallen asleep. Then the green light on his desk showed, and a bell tinkled gently. The call was from the managing director of one of Timbals' European subsidiaries. It was about some confusion over export deliveries and should have been dealt with by O'Rourke, but the managing director had asked specifically for Lowson. He applied emollient remarks, said that he hoped to be making a European tour later in the year, and sent for O'Rourke. He did not ring Paul back until nearly five o'clock.

"Paul, I think you've got the whole thing a bit out of perspective. Essentially the luncheon room's meant for the use of directors. When they've got guests." His laugh came warm, rich, easy. "Even directors aren't really supposed to use it unless they have guests, though I daresay some of them will."

"Blaney and O'Rourke aren't directors. That's just my point."

"No. But Blaney's on home marketing and O'Rourke handles exports. The way Brian put it to me is that they both often have guests from whom we're getting business, people who demand a bit of special treatment. *You* know. That's something you just can't say about Personnel."

"I see."

"Just have a word with me any time you've got guests who

seem to you to need the full treatment; I'll make sure you use the luncheon room."

"But my name doesn't go on the list?"

You shouldn't have said that, Lowson thought, you should have left it alone. "Paul, I don't mind bending the rules but I never break them. And they're not my rules, you know, they're Brian's, though I thought he was being quite reasonable."

At that point Paul did leave it, and said thank you very much. If I made a list of the things he's done wrong in dealing with that little matter, Bob Lowson thought, starting with talking to me about it at all, they would fill a page. But the satisfaction of his mood was too deep to be affected by petty annoyances.

The lift was packed. Paul found himself thigh to thigh with a middle-aged woman from Accounts. Joy Lindley, on the other side of the lift, smiled at him. As they walked toward the Underground she was a step or two behind him, and he stopped to let her catch up.

"It was very nice of you, Mr. Vane. Not telling Mr. Hartford about the memo."

"Think nothing of it." He asked questions and found out that she lived in Highgate with her family, that her mother had had an operation and was more or less an invalid, and that she would have liked to go to university but didn't get good enough grades. "I'm pretty stupid."

"Nonsense. You wouldn't have lasted a week in Brian Hartford's office if you were stupid." The presence of this long-legged filly cantering by his side made him feel youthful and frisky. At the Underground entrance he said, "Come and have a drink with me. Just a quick one."

Suddenly, unexpectedly, she put out her tongue at him, said, "Ask me tomorrow," waved and walked across the street. He was delighted. Later the wheels of the train rattled out words he had heard before: *Vane Vane, off again.* Not really, he told himself. I won't say another word to the little minx.

The place was just off the M4 near Datchet, a rambling Victorian country house approached by a winding drive of copper beeches. The evening was chilly, and no patients were in the grounds. Hartford went up to the first floor, spoke to the sister on duty.

"Good evening, Mr. Hartford. Not quite so well today, I'm afraid. But we have our ups and downs."

"Yes." His lips were pressed thinner than usual as he walked down the corridor. The card on the door said *Mrs. Ellen Hartford*. It was yellow, not white. His wife had been here for eight years.

She sat at a table by the window. From the door her profile looked like that of the girl he had married. It was not until you were close that the puffy cheeks and slack mouth became obvious. Her eyes were like dead cornflowers. They looked at Hartford without appearing to see him. He spoke her name, kissed her cheek. She brushed the cheek as though a fly had touched her, then made a gesture toward the gardens.

"Nobody out there now."

"No. It's fairly cold."

"But they've been there."

"You haven't been out yourself today?"

"They've been watching me. All the afternoon. Two of them, on patrol, up and down. Waiting to get in. Over that balcony." She made a gesture at the balcony outside her window. "But I have to watch, and I can't watch all the time. I must get some sleep."

"Of course."

"I want the balcony taken away. Knocked down. So that I'm safe."

He knew that it was foolish to argue, although for a long time he had tried to do so. Now he was silent. Her hands twined and retwined, a sure sign that she was more than usually disturbed.

"Have you got anything?"

He drew from his pocket a half-pound block of chocolate. She broke off a piece, ate it greedily. "They're trying to starve me here. Nothing to eat today since breakfast. You're not to say I'm lying; it's true." She put a hand up to her eyes as though afraid of being hit. "I don't like it here; I want to go back to Bayley."

Bayley was the village where they had lived before the accident. "I'll see what I can do."

"What?"

"I said I'll see. We'll talk about it again." He knew that in half an hour she would have forgotten the conversation.

"They may try to stop me, but I've made plans. Not silly ones. Shall I tell you about them? You're not listening."

"I am."

"I shan't tell you. Only that I've got a helper here. Somebody who is truly helpful. Or it seems she is. Only one thing that's wrong; it worries me. At some time or other she has offended God. She bears the mark. Do you know what God did to show his displeasure?" She leaned across. Her spittle touched his face. "He made her black."

Hartford looked at his watch. A little more than eight years ago she had been taking their ten-year-old daughter Eve to a party, had driven out of a side road without looking and run head on into a bus. Ellen had been badly concussed, and it had been some time before she could be told that Eve had been killed. She had found it impossible to cope with the simplest household tasks when she came out of the hospital, but it was six months before the extent of the damage to her brain was realized. For those six months he had kept her at home with a housekeeper to do the work, but when she set fire to the house he had accepted that she must go into a home. He was a logical man and liked to feel that he must "accept" facts, although of course it was she who had had to accept life in the home. Sometimes she would seem perfectly rational, but evenings like this one made him accept also that she would probably never come out. Perhaps, after all this time, he did not even want her to come out. She said something through a mouthful of chocolate.

"What's that?"

"You've been lying to me. You sold our house at Bayley. You live in a flat. You sold it because you wanted to keep me in here, didn't you?"

There would be another half hour of this. He always stayed for an hour, and he came three times a week. He now felt no emotion at all in relation to Ellen, but he sometimes wondered what Eve would have been like now, at eighteen, if she had lived.

During this month of June Anne Marie's elder sister, Nathalie, came over to England, and took her clothes and few other belongings back to France. She talked to Plender, who was impressed by her certainty that the girl would not have gone off without at least telling her family. They were Catholics, Anne Marie adored her father and got on well with her sister, and although Nathalie admitted that Anne Marie was rather flighty and occasionally did things they disapproved of, it was inconceivable that she would have run off and not been in touch with them.

Plender told Hurley, who was not much impressed. What, he wondered, were they expected to do about it that wasn't being done already? Details about her had been circulated, her name and description were on the Missing Persons list.

The sergeant ran a hand through his black curly hair. He was a conscientious young man, and he had been worrying about the case. "Maybe something has happened to her."

"Perhaps it has. I daresay she deserved it. What then?"

"It's those two disappearances, sir. I can't get over the idea that they're connected. We haven't heard anything of the other girl either."

But a couple of days later they did hear something of the other girl, in the form of a telephone call from Joan Brown's landlady, Mrs. Ransom. Joan Brown had turned up again, asking if her old room was still vacant. Mrs. Ransom had told her of the police inquiries, and Joan Brown herself came into the station.

Plender saw her. She was a dumpy girl in her middle or late

twenties, with no obvious attractions. Not the most likely candidate, Plender had to admit, for a sex crime. He told her that she had given them a lot of trouble.

"I don't understand. What have I done wrong?"

"I didn't say you'd done anything wrong, only that you'd caused a lot of trouble. Not only to us. Mr. Darling, your employer, came in to see us. He said you just left without giving notice or saying a word. Is that right?"

"I suppose so."

"That wasn't very considerate. Why did you do it?"

"He was an old pinchfist. It was rotten pay. And there wasn't much to do anyway, business was slack. I got fed up."

"So you left him, just packed your things and cleared off. Why?"

"I don't see it's your business."

"Boyfriend trouble?"

"I wanted a rest."

"Where did you go to?"

A pause. "Home. At Kiley. Just outside Mansfield. In Nottinghamshire." Flatly she repeated, "For a rest. Things were getting me down."

"Just suddenly like that, you needed a rest." Plender got along well with most women, but he was finding Joan Brown hard work. "And what have you come back for now?"

"Might as well be in Rawley as anywhere, I suppose."

"Are you going to ask for your old job back?"

"Shouldn't think so. I told you it was boring and he didn't pay much. I'll look around."

"Do you know a girl named Anne Marie Dupont? This girl." He showed her a photograph. He had the impression that her mind was occupied by some different subject, and decided that it was almost certainly connected with a young man, and that this was the reason for her leaving Rawley.

His eye automatically noted: no rings, nice hands but doesn't take care of them, worn handbag but it looks like leather and not plastic. There was a vague wild look in her eye that he associated with religion, on the slender basis that he had once had a girl friend with a similar look, and that she had become a Jehovah's Witness. He said on impulse, "Are you very religious, Miss Brown?"

At last he had something that interested her. "I was brought up a Methodist. But I don't go to chapel now."

"Is your father a preacher?"

"No, a schoolmaster. But they're both Methodists, very strict. What made you think I was?"

Plender said truthfully that she reminded him of a girl he knew who had joined the Jehovah's Witnesses, and her interest waned. She gave him her parents' address, and promised to let him know if she moved again in the next few weeks. Then she wandered out of the station as vaguely as she had come in.

He decided against ringing the parents. After all, what would he be ringing them for? As Joan Brown said, she had done nothing wrong. If she chose to pack in a job and leave Rawley because she wanted a rest or for some other reason, that was her affair. When he reported her visit to Hurley, the inspector made it clear that he was gallantly refraining from saying "I told you so."

So, with the Joan Brown disappearance cleared up, interest in Anne Marie Dupont dropped almost to vanishing point. Only Plender felt uneasily that perhaps something more should be done about it.

8

The Tennis Club

The centers of middle-class social life in Rawley were the Rotary Club and the golf club for men, the social club and the Townswomen's Guild for women, and the tennis club. The Rotary Club was for businessmen, the golf club for those on a rather higher social level including some Timbals executives, the social club (which included the bridge club that Alice Vane had joined) for their wives. Rawley was too big to be a company town, but there were five thousand workers at the Timbals factory, and the firm helped to support most of these organizations.

The tennis club was upon the whole the place where the sexes chiefly met, not just occasionally but all the time. The social grading there was not less accurate for being invisible and unmentioned. In theory anybody could join, but in practice the ordinary Timbals workers would no more have thought of trying to do so than would a grocer's shop assistant. They belonged to the firm's Sports Club, which had better courts than Rawley Tennis Club and more of them, available at a much lower cost. To join the club was, as Bob Lowson had said to Paul Vane, to keep in the swim—or rather, to swim in the right bath. Paul had taken his advice and joined. Jennifer had refused, on the ground that she'd finished with all that stuff at school; and Alice didn't

40

play. At the tennis club on a June evening he was the center of a trivial incident which was later to assume some importance.

Paul played tennis as he played other games, flashily rather than well. He had a hard first service which went in only occasionally, and an erratic whipped forehand drive. He was playing a mixed doubles with Louise Allbright against Ray Gordon and Sally Lowson. Ray and Sally should have been much too good for the other pair, but Sally was expressing her boredom with the Rawley scene by playing almost every stroke a few seconds late, as though she were in Copenhagen and operating her racket by remote control. Paul, on the other hand, was playing altogether above himself. At four–five down he won two points by decisive smashes to pull up from love–thirty on Louise's service to thirty–all. Then a third smash raised a puff of white on the back line. Ray called, "Out."

Paul said incredulously, "Out? I saw the chalk come up."

"Just dust. It was a foot out."

Thirty–forty. Louise served, Sally returned it near to the baseline, Paul hit a stylish forehand which Ray moved to play at, then checked himself. "Out," he called. "Game. And set."

Paul, at the back of the court, stood with hands on hips, then came up and spoke to Louise. They both laughed.

"What's the joke?"

"Nothing, nothing at all."

"There must have been, you were both laughing. Let me in on it." Ray too had now come up to the net. "Louise."

"Nothing. Paul just said—"

"Yes?"

She looked at Paul, who said, "It was just a casual remark. A joke."

Ray's neat face looked as if it were being screwed by a vise. "I should like to know what you said."

Before Paul could answer, Louise spoke. She had a delicate little-girl voice. "Paul said if you were taking one of those drunkenness tests where you have to walk along a white line you wouldn't pass it, because you wouldn't be able to see where the white line was. I thought it was rather funny. I mean, you know that last shot was in."

Ray glared at her, then walked off the court. "You shouldn't have said that," Paul said mildly.

"But it *was* in. Wasn't it, Sally?"

"I've no idea."

Paul put an arm round each of them. "Let's just simmer down, shall we?"

The girls were drinking gin and tonic and Paul a glass of beer when Ray came into the bar. When Paul asked what he was drinking he looked deliberately at him. "I don't drink with people who say I've cheated. Or with little bitches who try to make trouble."

He turned and walked out. He had not spoken loudly, but the barman had heard and so had Peter Ponsonby, who was standing only a couple of feet away. Peter's cherub cheeks trembled with indignation. "Such rudeness. It's intolerable. I do apologize to you both. I shall see that the Committee hears about it."

Paul said it was just a stupid joke that had been misunderstood, and Louise asked if she could have another drink. Sally went home soon afterward. When she got home she told her parents what had happened. She was campaigning for a flat in London which she would share with a girl friend, but so far her father had refused to stump up any money, saying that she could finish her trainee management course first. He said now that Paul seemed to have stepped out of line, and she replied that the club was so fantastically dull that anything which livened it up was welcome. She went on to say that it was no worse than the rest of Rawley. Then she went upstairs, slammed the door of her bedroom and played the latest James Taylor record much too loudly.

Paul and Louise stayed drinking and playing darts until ten o'clock. He was in good form at darts too, and after he had ended one game with a double, she hugged him closely. Then he drove her home, and kissed her good night outside her house. She kissed him back, then broke away. He sat with his fingers tapping the steering wheel.

"I'm too old, is that it? Or is it Ray?"

"Not really. I'm finished with him."

"You've got somebody else?"

"Could be," she said with devastating coyness. "Could be I shan't be in Rawley forever. I mean, it's dead, isn't it? For young people."

She was not particularly attractive but the words excited him, with the implication that they belonged to different worlds. He tried to drag her toward him with one arm and to put his other hand up her skirt. She pulled away, got out of the car and slammed the door. He watched her retreating back, started the car and went home.

That Sunday Paul and Alice went to dinner with her parents, who lived in the county, only a few miles away. When Paul had mentioned this as an inducement for going to live in Rawley, Alice was sharp.

"I shouldn't have thought you'd have wanted to see them more than twice a year. You know you hate them. And they don't love you."

"I get on perfectly well with your father." Alice's father had been a brigadier, and although his unit had been the Pay Corps and he was now retired, he still used the title. Her mother had spotted at once that Paul was not out of the top drawer, and had disapproved of him accordingly. There was a time when he had christened them the Brigadier and his lady, and Alice had found it funny, but that was long ago.

"You know Daddy never talks about anything but the weather."

"The trouble is that when you're with them you become a different person."

"How would you know what sort of person I am? You've never tried to find out."

He did not reply. This was as near as they ever got to quarreling.

When they arrived the Brigadier was in the garden prodding away with a hoe. He kissed his daughter, said to his son-in-law, "Hallo, young shaver," and added, "Need rain. Very dry."

In the house, Norah, the Brigadier's lady, met them with a jangle of bracelets, the offer of an enameled cheek, a glass of very dry sherry. At dinner she spoke of the servant problem. Alice, in tune with her mother, said that it was hopeless to try to get anybody in Rawley, they were all employed at the Timbals factory.

"What this country needs is a sharp dose of unemployment. It would bring people to their senses."

The Brigadier liked, as he said, to get his head down over his food, but now he lifted it. "Don't suppose you'd want too much of that, eh, Paul? Expect you get it, though. Seasonal work and all that."

"We try to avoid seasonal employment as much as we can. After all, it's my job to keep people happy. They aren't happy if they know they may be out of a job next month." He felt Norah's eyes upon him. Was he using the wrong tools?

"A personnel man. I've always thought that was a strange occupation," she said. "It's what your army units used to be called, personnel." With no change of tone she said to Paul, "I think you need another knife."

It was true. He had used a knife instead of a spoon for the melon.

The evening went on like that. When he drove back Alice said, "You hated every minute. Why did you say we should go?"

"You were no help. You just echoed your mother."

"We're not compatible," she said softly into the darkness of the car. She imagined that dark young man at her side.

9

Departure of an Odd Girl

On June 22, a Wednesday, Plender was idly going around an exhibition in the Market Square called *Crime Prevention— It's Up To You.* The exhibition was a traveling one, staffed by some London men who managed not to smile when Plender said he was from Rawley CID and was hoping to find out something new about catching villains. He was standing in front of an exhibit full of flashing differently colored lights, which was meant to show the chain of communications between crime squads, when he heard his name called. He turned and saw Ray Gordon of the *Rawley Enquirer.* Plender grinned. "Don't quote me, but I'm trying to learn a bit about my trade."

"What's it worth to say you weren't here?"

"I'll buy you a beer, if that's what you mean. You can tell me the latest dirt."

"Let me buy you one. As a matter of fact, I was thinking of giving you a ring."

"To report a crime?"

"Hope not." Plender thought of Gordon as a man with plenty of nerve, but in the bar of the Red Lion he seemed almost nervous. "A girl I know has disappeared. Her parents asked me not to say anything about it, but still."

"When?"

"Went out on Monday evening, didn't come back."

"Your girl friend, was she? Had a row with her, anything like that?"

"She wasn't my girl friend. I've taken her out a couple of times, but nothing serious. And we did have a bit of a squabble last Saturday at the tennis club. She was playing with a conceited bastard called Vane, just come to live here, and we had a few words. Nothing really. I hadn't seen her since. Her mother gave me a call yesterday, to see if I'd heard from her."

"So she lives at home. How old?"

"Nearly nineteen."

"Doing a bit of cradle snatching, weren't you?"

Ray's embarrassment deepened. "Sounds like that, I daresay, but she could look after herself. Well, in a way. She didn't exactly want sex, she wanted adventure, but she was afraid too, if you know what I mean. The tennis club wasn't her line, much too respectable and unexciting, but she'd have been frightened to go out for anything else. She was an odd girl, I suppose."

"Have you made her?"

"None of your bloody business."

Plender said pacifically, "I'm just trying to find out whether she slept around."

"I'm sure she didn't. She told me she'd slept with a boy at some pop festival last year, but my guess would be that was about it. No, I didn't make her."

Plender ordered another beer. "Know any details? I mean, where she was going on Monday night, that kind of thing? No? All right, where do the parents live?"

"Eighty Woodside Place. Look, if you're going round to see them, try to forget I told you about this, will you? They won't like it."

"What do you expect me to say, cock—that I'm calling at every house down their road to find out how many daughters are missing? What's she doing, just being a homebody?"

"Left school, got a place at some university up north, couldn't make up her mind whether she wanted to take it up." He brooded on his beer. "I suppose you could say she was filling in time waiting for something to happen."

"A lot of us are doing that."

Plender went around to Woodside Place, which was a large estate of neat identical modern houses built in the form of a letter E. It took him some time to find number 80. The doorbell had a two-tone chime.

The small woman who opened the door had a dumpling face and boot button eyes which flared with fear or anxiety when Plender gave his name. She ushered him in quickly, as though he were a rent collector. In the back room a tall man with a toothbrush mustache was watching television.

"Dad, this is Mr. Plender. From the police. This is my husband. Dad, turn it off."

Allbright rose, took reluctant steps toward the box while still staring at it, turned the switch. The picture vanished. His wife said, "It's about Louise, isn't it?"

"I haven't got any news of her. I wondered if you'd heard anything. She left on Monday, is that right?"

"Beer," Allbright said. "You'll have a drink . . . Inspector, is it?"

"Sergeant."

Mrs. Allbright went out, returned with two cans of beer and two glasses. Allbright poured, raised his glass in greeting, drank. "You may think we should have been in touch before, but you've got to consider my position. I can't afford to be made a laughingstock."

"What is your position?" Plender asked politely.

"I'm at Timbals. Assistant works supervisor, Moldings Division." He puffed out his chest as though a medal were on it.

"And why would you be a laughingstock?"

He looked incredulous. "What . . . if it got to be known George Allbright can't control his own daughter?" He paused.

"Here, if you've got no news of her, how d'you know she's gone?"

"A friend of hers told me. You can't keep this kind of thing quiet."

Allbright spoke bitterly. "That dirty little journalist. It's all they ever think of, publicity."

"But, Dad, he only did it for the best." His wife was timid but determined. "What George thinks is, she's done the same as before."

"And what was that?"

"Last year, when she wanted to go to the Isle of Wight pop festival."

"And what happened?"

"Told her she couldn't go," Allbright said. "Might as well have been talking to the air; she just went. Forty-eight hours away, no message. We were worried sick. Then she just turned up again, cool as you please."

"She did leave a message, Dad; it was just that poster got put on top of it." He waved a hand irritably, went out of the room. "We did go to the police that time. We felt such fools when she just turned up and asked what all the fuss had been about. But you mustn't get the wrong idea—she's not one of those rebels you're always hearing about. She just doesn't get on with Dad, that's all. Of course I can see he's got his position to keep up, but all that trouble about wearing minis. Everybody wears them now, I told him. I don't care what *everybody* does, he says, Louise's my daughter."

"What about boyfriends?"

"Never seemed to have them, or she never brought them home. There was this Ray Gordon; he took her out two or three times and once brought her back here. Then on Saturday night she said one of the bosses at Timbals wanted to make love to her, but she wouldn't let him."

"What was his name, do you remember?"

"A Mr. Vane. Mind you, she may have said it just to spite her dad. But she was always talking about what she'd do, the kind of life she'd live when she got away from here. Don't be in such a hurry, I said, you'll soon be at college."

"Where did she go on Monday?"

"To a Keep Fit class at the Institute." Tears came from the boot button eyes. "Oh, Mr. Plender, I'm so worried."

A lavatory flushed. Allbright returned with more beer.

"No more for me, thanks. Two things. Have you got a photograph of her? And could I see her room before I go?"

Mrs. Allbright said nervously, "Dad?"

"I suppose so, I bloody well suppose so. She's my daughter, you know; I've got my feelings too. But I'm not going to be made a fool of, and I'm not going to have my name spread over the papers with stories about Hunt for Missing Girl when it's all a load of bloody rubbish. My principle is the young don't know as much as their fathers and mothers, and they ought to do what they're told. Right, eh, Sergeant?"

Plender, who thought nothing of the kind, said, "Right."

Mrs. Allbright went through a box of photographs, and Plender chose a head-and-shoulders. The picture showed a girl with straight long hair, wide-set eyes and an undecided expression. She was far from beautiful, but there was something attractive about the face.

He could not have said what he expected to find in the girl's bedroom, but his five-minute look around revealed nothing helpful. Tennis rackets, pinups of Mick Jagger and other pop stars, romantic novels and a couple of books about Buddhism, school textbooks; there was nothing out of the way. He found no correspondence. Mrs. Allbright followed every step he took, rather as though Louise might be produced from a drawer or the wardrobe. She couldn't be sure whether any clothes were gone, but she didn't think so. No suitcase had been taken, although Louise had with her the blue carryall she always took to the Keep Fit classes, and she could have put something in that.

By the time he left she was slightly distraught. Plender told her not to worry.

"What will you do now?"

"Tell my inspector."

When he left the TV was on again.

Hurley was not greatly impressed. Disappearances of this kind, he repeated, were two a penny. "What have you got after all, Harry? We'd never have thought anything about the French piece if it hadn't been for what's her name, Brown. Then Brown turns up. Now you've got another; that's only two. There are a lot of girls in Rawley."

"Do you mean we should just leave it?"

"Of course not, I didn't say that. Ask some questions. Quietly though, tactfully."

After Plender had gone, Hurley pondered. He ought to cover himself in case the two disappearances were actually connected. He sent a memo through to Detective Chief Inspector Hazleton at Divisional HQ. Rawley contained two sub-Divisions, Rawley and Burnt Over, and Hurley was in charge of Rawley sub-Division. The arrangement was rather artificial, because Divisional HQ was in the same building, and although Rawley was a town it had no separate police force. Hurley could easily have gone in to see Hazleton, but he was a great believer in getting things down on paper.

The Rawley Adult Educational Institute ran classes in everything from aeronautics and beekeeping to weight lifting and zoology. Plender asked for the Keep Fit class, and was directed to Miss Weston in room 24. There he found twenty women in shorts and T-shirts swinging their bodies about. Several of them were middle-aged. Breasts flopped and stomachs trembled. Miss Weston, lithe and slim, set an example. Music played, Miss Weston and her acolytes chanted, devotees of an ancient ritual. "Hup-two-three, down-two-three, left-two-three, right-two-three," they breathed in unison. Some of them saw Plender and stopped, evidently glad of the break. Miss Weston became aware of an alien presence. She turned to him, hands on hips. Plender proffered his card. She barely glanced at it.

"Didn't they tell you in the office that men aren't allowed in the classroom? You're interrupting rhythm maintenance."

"Sorry. I didn't know police counted as men. I wanted to speak to you about Louise Allbright."

"I'll be free in ten minutes."

He stood outside reading the notices on the board advertising the Institute dances, film club, debating society, dramatic society and hikers' group. The women came out, transformed into Rawley housewives. Then Miss Weston, thin and wiry, hair pulled back. They went to the canteen and ordered cups of tea.

"Louise Allbright was in your class. Did she come on Monday?" She nodded. "Anything special about her that evening?"

"Why?"

Miss Weston, breastless and heavy browed, looked like an aggressive and, if you cared for such looks, attractive boy. Plender, who preferred round soft girls, found her slightly antipathetic, but he smiled. "Keep this to yourself, there may be nothing in it. The class was six-thirty to seven-thirty; she should have gone home after it. She didn't, and she hasn't been back since. Now, was there anything special?"

"She was excited. I don't know what about."

"How well did you know her?"

"Better than anyone else in the class, but that doesn't mean much. She'd been coming for two terms, so I'd seen a bit of her. She was unhappy at home, you know that? Her father was an awful bastard. She wanted to get away." She chewed her lip. "I told her she could move in with me if she wanted."

Were lesbian inclinations being suggested? "But she didn't."

"No. She was keen to get to London to live. So she said. She had some sort of vision of herself doing what she thought were romantic things in the big city. You know, most of them come to class because they're overweight and think they can cut down by exercise while they go on stuffing themselves with pastries. Bloody fools. But Louise did it because she wanted to have a perfect body. She was a bit thick in the hips. She once said to me that she'd like to be a striptease dancer. The point is she wouldn't—wouldn't have liked it, I mean. Basically she wanted romance, not sex. She liked to think of herself as bohemian, but she was respectable as hell." This time there could be no doubt about the meaning of her tight-lipped smile.

"Any boys around? Did she ever talk about one in particular?"

"Talked about them. I don't know if it went any further. This term it was one called Ray something. Journalist, I think."

"Those gym suit things they were wearing. Do they bring them along?"

"Yes. They have carryalls, small cases, that kind of thing."

"No lockers? No? All right. Anything more you can think of that might be useful? No idea what she was excited about on Monday?"

"The odds are it was a man." Miss Weston's smile was tight. "That doesn't mean a man was poking her. She was a timid girl who wished she was different, is that any help?"

"Not a bit," Plender said cheerfully. "But thanks all the same."

Hazleton's office was bigger than Hurley's, and cooler, partly because an electric fan hummed in it. Hurley's shirt was sticking to his body, and he envied Hazleton the electric fan. The DCI's voice on the telephone had been sharp, but Hurley faced him with the imperturbability of the lazy man who feels sure that he has covered any tracks indicating possible negligence.

"These two disappearances. What have you been doing about them?"

"We only heard about the second one yesterday. Plender's been looking into it. So far he hasn't come up with much. The girl had been talking about becoming a striptease dancer."

52

"And the first case, the French au pair? Why wasn't I told about that at the time?"

The DCI was a big man with a face that appeared to be all knobs—two for his cheekbones, another for his nose, and an outsize knob for his formidable chin. When he was moved emotionally the knobs all shone, and they were shining now. Hurley saw that he had better choose his words with care.

"Didn't seem necessary to worry you with it specially. Most likely thing is she's gone off to try her luck in London. She wasn't on very good terms with the family she worked for."

Hazleton liked to say that he could smell when something was cooking, and he smelled it now. Perhaps the dish might be of interest to Charlie Hazleton? Well, perhaps, but still his prime emotion was of anger at something approaching slackness. "A girl disappears, doesn't take her clothes, doesn't leave any message, and you do nothing about it. I think very little of that, Inspector."

"With respect, sir, we did do something. We talked to everybody involved. And she's on Missing Persons."

"You did the least you possibly could." His glare did not invite a reply. "Now another girl's gone. I want you to find out where this second one has got to, you understand? What did she do after she left this Keep Fit class, did anyone see her later Monday night, did a car pick her up, was this row with the journalist more serious than he makes out? Treat it as possible rape or murder. And one more thing."

"Yes?"

"Don't let that journalist get to hear about the French girl so that he can splash it in the *Enquirer.* If the time comes to make a statement we'll do it ourselves."

The investigation turned up one thing of interest immediately. Louise had been seen after the Keep Fit class ended. At eight-fifteen she had attended a meeting of the Film Society at the Institute. She was a member, but had been only once before during the term. The secretary knew and recognized her, but beyond saying that she was there could not be much help. She had been at the film show, that was all, and had come in and gone out alone. There had been a horror film, one in a season that the Society was running, and it had been well attended.

After the show ended at nine forty-five another girl who knew Louise said that she thought she had seen her in company with a woman just outside the Institute gates, but she could not be sure. She had only seen their backs and could not even be certain that it was Louise, except that she had the same sort of long hair. After that she had disappeared completely. And why had she gone to the show at all? Because she was specially interested in horror films? To meet somebody? Apparently not. To fill in time? It hardly seemed likely.

Two days later her disappearance made headlines in the national press when a blue carryall was found on top of a London bus in Charing Cross Road. The finder took it to the Lost and Found department. The carryall contained a gym suit and shoes, and also a handbag with the usual impedimenta in it— mirror, handkerchief, powder, cigarettes and matches, a key. The carryall and bag were sent down to Rawley, and the Allbrights identified them as belonging to their daughter. The key was the key of the front door. Only one unusual thing was found in the handbag. A fragment of an envelope had been caught in the lining. The material of the envelope was similar to what could be bought in a thousand shops. On the back of this fragment, however, somebody had printed in ink "E 203." That, for what it was worth, was the only tangible clue to Louise Allbright's disappearance.

10

Job Enrichment and Lavatories

Bob Lowson always spared ten minutes from dictation, when he traveled up to town, to look at the morning papers. On this morning he said to Sally, who traveled up with him, "Didn't you say something about a girl named Louise Allbright? At the tennis club."

She usually read the paper herself in the car, but on this day she had spent the journey looking out of the window. "Yes."

"I never forget a name," he said with satisfaction. "She's disappeared. Look at this."

The headline said: HAVE YOU SEEN THIS GIRL? Below it was a smudgy picture of Louise and an account of her disappearance. Sally barely glanced at it.

"You don't seem much interested."

"I didn't know her well."

"Isn't she the girl you were playing doubles with last weekend? When you said there was a bit of an argument, and Paul was mixed up in it."

"Yes."

"Then I should have thought you'd be interested. You do still live in Rawley, you know."

"He took her home that evening. Paul Vane."

"What's that supposed to mean?" Her father's porcine good humor had disappeared.

55

"Nothing. I was just reminding you. Since you're interested."

"Then you can just shut up about it. The less said about that kind of thing the better."

The paper on Paul Vane's desk, done in neat facsimile typewriting, was headed: "Job Enrichment at Timbals Plastics. A Study in Deliberate Method Change Planning. By E. K. Malendine, Ph.D." Esther Malendine was the woman he had mentioned to Alice, who had been appointed as his assistant. After getting a degree in Logic and Social Science at a fashionable university she had gone straight out to the United States, where she had worked for some enormous corporation. At the time he had been rather in favor of her appointment. It had sounded a good idea for him to have a woman assistant, although he had been disconcerted at first sight of Esther, who wore glasses with enormous smoky lenses, and had a formidable academic manner. Since then he had realized his mistake. Now his heart sank as he looked at the first couple of pages:

The belief expressed by Weinstein, Bauer and other behavioral scientists in the potentialities of job enrichment has proved fully justified by the results obtained in the American multilevel PJC Corporation among others . . . job enrichment is essentially participatory, it is unitary and not divisive, it implies the fulfillment of individual potential without losing the advantages of mechanization and computerization, it might be called an individual shaping of mechanization. . . . Deliberate Method Change (DMC hereafter) applied within a structure like Timbals would involve teams from each area of our operation devising their own scheme for Work Simplification . . . the philosophy of job enrichment can be summarized in the Seven Movements . . .

He settled down to read the whole thing, and when he had finished went along to Esther's office. She was talking into a recorder, and he heard the phrase "avoidance of infinite variables" before she switched off. He had decided to be pleasant.

"I haven't had a chance yet to go through your paper in detail, Esther, but it looks like a fine job of work." She gazed at him through the enormous glasses. "I just wonder whether it isn't going to be a bit above the heads of some of the people who read it."

"I don't think so. Job enrichment is a familiar concept in most big firms now. The problem is to get the board to accept it."

"You don't feel it could be put more simply? It seems to me job enrichment just means getting people to use a bit of initiative. We're trying to do that all the time."

"Rather an oversimplification. But in any case that implies DMC. And a preliminary would have to be the setting up of work study groups."

He retained the pleasantness of his manner, although with some difficulty. "Esther, I knew you were preparing a memorandum, but this is more like a thesis. If you were going to do something on this scale you should have had a word with me first, and we could have talked about it in detail."

"Brian Hartford suggested I should prepare it. He's very interested in group communication method projects."

It was like talking to a multisyllabled computer. Back in his office he spoke to Hartford.

"I think you might have had a word with me first, I must say. She's my assistant, and this must have taken up a lot of time. We're under considerable pressure already."

"I'm sorry if you think I've infringed protocol," Hartford said. "I believe actually she wrote most of it at home. But she's come up with some interesting ideas, don't you agree?"

"A good deal of it is hot air, and most of the rest we knew already." He regretted the words as soon as they were spoken.

"I'm sorry you feel like that," Hartford said neutrally. "We'll be considering the report at a board meeting next week. I shall look forward to hearing your views."

Paul sent for his secretary and began to dictate some letters, but found that he was repeating himself and stumbling over words. In' the end he left her to answer most of the mail herself.

Sally was working in the Sales Division (Toys) for a few weeks. After that she would go on to Sales Division (Domestic) and then to Sales Division (Foreign). The people she worked with knew that she was the managing director's daughter. Sales manager (toys) treated her almost with deference, and most of the other people in the division kept out of her way. She had only one friend, Pamela Wilberforce, who wrote copy in Publicity. They met as they often did, in the rest room.

Pamela was twenty-five, a self-assured blonde whose toughness was part of her attraction for Sally. She had already, as she was fond of saying, mislaid one husband, and meant to try out a lot of men before taking on another.

"What's up?" she asked. "You look like a bit of classroom chalk."

"Louise has disappeared. It's in the paper."

"Who the hell's Louise?"

"That girl at Rawley; you remember I told you I'd shown the mag to her and she was fascinated. She wrote a letter to that man, the one who wrote to you."

"So. What then?"

"The day she disappeared, I don't know, but I think she was going to meet him. Oh, Pam, suppose something's happened to her through me."

"Of course nothing's happened."

"What do you think I ought to do?"

"Nothing. Just don't get in a tizzy."

"I'd never forgive myself if anything had happened because of me. You know, I used to laugh at her a bit. I planted her on that journalist."

"You mean the one you said had hands like wet gloves." Sally felt better after listening to Pam. It was nice to be with a girl who never lost her cool. "Look, sweetie pie, you've got to calm down. And it just so happens I've got a calmer with me."

At first Sally refused the joint, because she had only tried them a couple of times and was not at all sure that she liked the effect, but in the end she accepted it, and it was blissful. They sat in their cubicles talking, taking puffs, getting up to pass it over. Then Pam called, "Hey, Sally. Come and look."

"What?"

58

"In here." Sally went in. "Look. Filthy." There was certainly a line of dirt around the washbasin. "And no lav paper."

"So there isn't. Perhaps someone's pinched it."

"Disgraceful."

"It is disgraceful."

"I'll tell you what it is—they don't look after the loos properly any more. Let's look in the others."

In two compartments out of seven there was no lavatory paper. In one the lavatory bowl was choked with it. "Disgraceful and disgusting," Pam said. "You have to do something about something, do something about that."

"How d'you mean?"

"You're the old man's daughter, you've got influence. You've always said."

"I do have influence. Dad listens to me."

"You ought to talk to him."

"I'll talk to him."

Pam tore off half a roll of paper, stuffed it down a lavatory. "Make it good. And, sweetie pie."

"Yes?"

"You talk to your old man about that flat. We'd have fun, I tell you, real humming fun."

When Sally got back to the office she rang her father at once. He was out of the room, and she spoke to his secretary. Five minutes later he rang back. He was not pleased, asking what all this nonsense was about dirty lavatories. She still felt as if she were treading on clouds, but they were clearing a little. She spoke carefully, hearing her own words.

"It isn't nonsense. They're awful. In three of them there's no paper."

"Then go and tell the head of your department."

"All the girls think it's awful. They don't like to say anything."

"Oh."

"I don't believe . . . don't believe they're ever cleaned now." She closed her eyes. She could have fallen asleep easily. She murmured, "Thought I should tell you."

Her father said in a slightly mollified tone, "I'll have it looked into. But I don't want you running to me with tales out of school, you understand."

He spoke to his efficient secretary. After lunch he found on his desk a complete report on the lavatory situation. In ten toilets there was no paper, and four of them were not working for one reason or another. The general cleanliness of the washrooms left something to be desired. It was suspected that a little mild vandalism had been going on, in the form of stealing toilet rolls or stuffing them down lavatories. Cleaning had been done daily until three months ago, when it had been changed to every other day. The change had been made on instructions from the Personnel Department. Lowson spoke to Paul Vane.

"Paul, did you give instructions for lavatory cleaning to be cut down?"

"What's that?" Not surprisingly, he sounded startled. Then he said, "That's right."

"What was the idea?"

"We had a memo round about cutting expenses. I put this up as a possible cut, and it was accepted."

"It doesn't seem to be working out too well. There've been complaints about the state of women's washrooms, and in some cases they seem to be justified."

"They ought to have come to me."

"I just happened to hear about them."

"If Personnel has the responsibility for looking after washrooms, then complaints should be made through heads of departments. And they should speak to me, not go behind my back. Has Brian Hartford got anything to do with this?"

To his astonishment Lowson heard a note of hysteria in the personnel director's voice. "Brian? Of course not. What made you think that?"

"I just thought he might have, that's all."

"There's no question of going behind your back. Or of blaming you, either. This was a reasonable attempt to cut corners that seems to be causing a bit of trouble, that's all. Can we go back to the old system from next week?"

"Yes."

"Then let's do that. The saving doesn't justify causing staff trouble."

"I'll make a note of it." Before Lowson could hang up he went on. "Have you seen Esther Malendine's paper? About job enrichment."

"It's on my desk. I haven't looked at it yet."

"I understand Hartford asked her to do it. She produced it without consulting me. I should like to make clear that it's purely a personal view of her own. As personnel director there's very little of it that I go along with. And I do resent the fact that it's been produced behind my back."

"I'm glad you told me," Bob Lowson said. The remark was the reverse of the truth. It was all trivial stuff, complaints by and about Paul Vane, but the total effect was a little disturbing. He riffled the pages of the report, and started to glance through it.

At lunchtime Paul Vane had one drink more than usual, and when on his return he met Joy Lindley in a corridor he stopped and spoke to her. They went that evening to a pub that he knew people from Timbals did not use.

"You're looking prettier than ever, Joy." It was the kind of remark he had been making to women for nearly twenty years. In fact the best thing about her was her legs, but she had that elixir of youth which in the last decade he had become more and more anxious to drink.

"I thought you'd forgotten me."

"That wouldn't be possible." They were sitting on bar stools, and he put a hand on her knee. "How are things? Are you happy in your work?"

"Miss Popkin's back now, and she's a bit of a trial, always going on about this and that. And Mr. Hartford's all right, I suppose, but he never says if he likes anything you've done, only if there's something wrong. I mean, it's as though what he'd really like is for you to be a machine." She took Paul's hand off her knee and put it on the bar. "And I'm not a machine."

"That's very interesting." He knew that he ought not to be talking in this way to a girl who worked for Brian Hartford,

but he plunged on. "Do you know my assistant, Esther Malendine?"

"The one with those funny glasses? She doesn't come into the
office much, but she's always talking to Mr. Hartford on the
phone. She's terribly clever, isn't she? I mean, terribly interested in all sorts of new ideas. I can't understand half of them,
but then my mum always did say I was a bit dim."

"I'll tell you something, Joy. I can't understand them either."
He felt a glow of pleasure at the way she talked, calling her
mother "mum." Why, she might be fourteen, and in the exhila-
ration of the moment he felt that he was no older. "Perhaps I'm
a bit dim too."

She stayed another half hour, and had one more drink. He
told her a bit about the problems of being personnel director
in an organization like Timbals. "The great thing is to remember that the group's made up of people, and you have to deal
with those people as individuals. It's no use talking to them
about work study methods; they don't know what you mean."
She nodded, wide-eyed. He did not put his hand on her knee
again.

Alice spent the afternoon playing bridge. In fact, she spent all
her afternoons now playing bridge. When she and Paul had first
married they had played a little, what is sometimes called
honeymoon bridge, but now she found subtleties and refine-
ments in the game that she had not known to exist. She got
bridge books out of the library, and played through at home the
games and problems given as examples in the newspapers. She
also began to smoke, not cigarettes but small cigars, which she
often kept in her mouth until they had gone out.

At first Penelope had been her partner, but Penelope could
not be bothered to remember which cards had fallen, and was
liable to be led into erratic calls or responses by inability to keep
her mind on the game. Alice now played regularly with blue-
rinsed, sharp-nosed Mrs. Clancy Turnbull, whose husband was
the director of an insurance company. Mrs. Clancy Turnbull
was a chain smoker of cigarettes. The concentration of both

women was terrifying to see, or at least it terrified Penelope, who felt like a hen that has taken an eaglet under her wing.

She told Dick something of this one evening. She had left the club at teatime (they had another au pair after all, so there was no need to hurry home), and Alice had seemed hardly to recognize her when she said good-bye.

"Unstable type." Dick got his pipe going. "Some sort of stress condition. Early menopause, very likely."

"What, at her age?"

"Can come at any age. Get all sorts of ideas and habits. Start thinking your husband's a pork chop and you don't fancy pork. Extreme concentration on a particular idea or subject isn't unusual."

"I'm worried about her, Dick. It seems so . . . abnormal. I mean, she wasn't even interested in bridge."

Like most psychologists, Dick considered normality such an illusory concept that he was not disturbed by departures from it. "Nothing to be done. May even be a good thing, give her something to think about. Once women start behaving oddly they're liable to go on doing it for years."

When Paul got home it was to find Jennifer washing up things in the kitchen, making a tremendous clatter. Alice was setting the table. She said that Jennifer was in a mood, and this was quickly confirmed.

"I come home in that filthy train, having to stand all the way, and the breakfast things haven't even been washed up. Do you know what she's been doing all day? Playing bridge. I can tell you I'm fed up with it."

"Now, Jen." He put an arm around her shoulders. He was a man who found something comforting in bodily contact. "I smell something cooking."

"Pork chops. You may have to live in Rawley, but I don't. I'm getting a flat in London."

Alice came in. She gave the impression of floating rather than walking.

"A couple of girls at work will come in with me. We've got

one lined up. Twenty pounds a week, we split it three ways. You won't have to subsidize me, don't worry. I'll be going at the end of the week."

Alice must have heard, but she did not give the impression that she was listening. She floated out again without comment. Jennifer turned the pork chops. "I can't help it; I have to get away."

"I'm not arguing." The whole scene contrasted jarringly with that delightful chat in the pub. "I hope we'll see something of you. Don't cut yourself off."

"I expect I'll be down most weekends." She bent down to take plates from the oven. "You'll look after her, won't you? I don't think she likes it much down here."

When he asked her about this after supper, when Jennifer had gone to her room, Alice said that she was perfectly content. Nor was she upset about Jennifer leaving. "She must do what she wants. But don't worry about me; I have the bridge club. I know several people there."

He watched with distaste as she lighted a cigar. "You used not to smoke."

"And now I do. And I play bridge. Do you object?"

"I suppose not."

"You should face the fact that in many ways we are simply incompatible."

There seemed no answer to this. He said that they must do a show in London next week, and she assented, but again he had the feeling that she was not listening. Later he watched TV. She took out a book called *100 Bridge Problems for Advanced Players*, got a pack of cards and lighted one of her cigars. Later they went upstairs and lay unspeaking in their separate beds.

Joy Lindley's father worked in the architect's department of the Greater London Council. He liked to hear about things that happened in Joy's office, and she often gave him a slightly embroidered account of life there. She told him now about the personnel director taking her out to drinks.

"He's ever so nice. I mean, quite old, but you'd never guess it from his clothes and you can talk to him, I mean, just as if he was someone about twenty-five. Of course I suppose being personnel director makes a difference. I mean, you've got to get on with people. Mr. Vane's very good at that."

Mrs. Lindley had an arthritic condition that kept her more or less immured in an armchair, from which she rose only with the aid of a stick. Like many invalids she had an enormous appetite, and also a tenacious memory for misfortune and catastrophe. Now she paused with a piece of pork pie from the tray in front of her halfway to her mouth. "What name did you say, Joy?"

"Who? Oh, Mr. Vane. I think his name's Paul. Yes, that's right."

"Edgar." Mr. Lindley, who had been listening with placid pleasure to Joy's recital, looked startled. "Get my letter file from the bedroom."

Edgar never queried his wife's requests, but did as he was told. The file contained all the correspondence she wished to preserve: her battle with the electricity company over an account, the complaints to the Council about a new housing development uncomfortably near their home, the angry correspondence with other members of the family about things that should have been left to her in an aunt's will. Now she went slowly through the file until she found a particular bundle of letters. The pork pie was pushed aside. "Edgar."

He had watched with apprehension. Abandonment of food meant something serious. "My dear."

"You must ring your sister Hetty. At once." She contemplated the tray in front of her, and said with satisfaction, "I shan't want any more supper."

11

Conference

The problem of Louise Allbright had now passed far beyond the range of Hurley, who had received such savage rebukes that he wished he had never heard her name. The people present at the conference called to discuss it at County HQ in Markstone, ten miles from Rawley, were the top brass of the county police. Hazleton was there from Rawley, with Detective Chief Superintendent Paling from County HQ, and the chief constable, Sir Felton Dicksee. The most important question to be settled was whether the County should handle the investigation, or whether they should call in Scotland Yard.

Sir Felton turned over the papers and reports in front of him. His dislike of paper work was well known. His friends said that he was essentially a man of action, his enemies that he was unable to read. "Never mind all this bumph," he said now. "The thing is, where are we, Paling? What have we got?"

Angus Paling put his fingertips together. His fingers were long and narrow. They were in keeping with a long narrow body and a long narrow head, with a cock's comb of silver hair. There was a sort of fastidiousness about Paling which irritated Hazleton, who thought that he was not much of a working copper. At the same time, Hazleton grudgingly admitted that he knew how to talk.

"The crucial thing, as I see it, is the discovery of the carryall and bag. Unless Louise left it on the bus by accident, which is so unlikely that we can rule it out, we must accept that something has happened to her. Accept that and there are two possibilities. Either she went up to London and whatever happened occurred there, or the carryall was deliberately planted in that bus to take attention away from Rawley."

Thank you for a statement of the blindingly obvious, Hazleton thought. Sir Felton said quite so, the thing was whether they were happy to deal with it themselves. Paling arched his silver eyebrows and looked at Hazleton, who recognized an old tactic of the DCS. Hazleton would express an opinion. Paling would say that he was prepared to go along with what had been suggested. If everything worked out well Paling would take most of the credit, if not Hazleton would get all of the blame. But still, Hazleton knew what he wanted, and he was prepared to go out on a limb to get it.

"My feeling, sir, is that we can handle it best down here. I don't think there's any doubt that whatever happened started in Rawley. Somebody here was responsible for her disappearance, whether she went up to London or not. There's an advantage in having our own men asking questions. They know the territory, and they know what to ask. And they know the people. We can look after it."

A bell rang. Sir Felton said, "Excuse me, gentlemen." The sound came from the watch on his wrist. He stopped it, got out of his chair and did a series of brisk exercises which began with a knee bend and ended with some quite violent arm and body swings. Hazleton, who had heard about these performances but never quite believed in them, watched in astonishment. Paling remained unmoved.

"Three times a day." Sir Felton sat down again. "Now, where are we? You want to keep it in the family. Paling?"

"There's a lot in what Chief Inspector Hazleton says. At the same time we have to face the fact that we've turned up nothing very useful so far. A couple of confessions with the facts hopelessly wrong, and the usual crop of people who saw her getting into a car, dragged into a car and so on. One woman who saw her beating at a window in a house trying to get out—that turned out to be a woman having a row with her husband. So far it's a load of nothing, isn't that so?" Hazleton nodded. Paling held up a thin hand as though to forestall objections, which were in fact not being made. "I'm sure everything possible is being done. That film show, for instance, seems to me important. Louise went to that quite out of the blue instead of going home. Why? We've talked to all the members the secretary can remember as being present." He made a gesture toward the papers in front of the chief constable. "Without result, except that the secretary says she was looking round as though she expected to meet somebody who hadn't turned up. Say that was so, how does it help? There is a case, I don't say more than that, for taking further steps."

Hazleton said doggedly, "Calling in the Yard, you mean? I still say we can handle it."

Paling was not going to be caught in a definite expression of opinion. "I don't want for a moment to express any lack of confidence."

The chief constable looked from one to the other of them. He knows what's happening, Hazleton thought, he's not a fool. "Right, then. It seems to me we're agreed. We keep it in the family. Good. Hazleton."

"Yes, sir."

"This journalist who knew her, Gordon. You've checked on him? Nothing in that?"

"I don't think so, sir. I gather from Gordon that he only took her out a couple of times, rather on the rebound from another girl at the club named Sally Lowson. It seems that he was keener on this Lowson girl than she was on him, and she suggested he might give Louise Allbright a turn. No serious attachment."

"Bob Lowson's daughter. Talked to her, have you?"

"Not yet, sir. The connection's a bit remote."

"She knew the Allbright girl though. Might be an idea to talk to her. I'll have a word with Bob Lowson, explain it to him."

The telephone rang. Paling took the call and passed the receiver to Hazleton. The DCI listened, said a few words, made a note. He put down the receiver, looked again at the note, spoke.

"That may be something interesting. A girl who saw Louise getting out of a car about ten-fifteen that night. More promising than usual; the girl was at school with her."

"Why hasn't she come forward before?" Paling asked.

"Away on holiday, didn't read the papers."

"Where did she see her? In Rawley?"

"No, outside. High Ashley." They looked at each other. High Ashley was a village in the heart of the downs that lay between Rawley and the coast. "She was with a woman. And she looked as though she was drunk."

12

Extracts from a Journal

━━ ━━ ━━ ━━ ━━ ━━ ━━ ━━ ━━ ━━ ━━ ━━ ━━ ━━ ━━ ━━

JUNE

I write at a time when my whole life has been changed, a time after the two Great Events. These are real, they are etched in my memory with the corrosion of acid or the splendor of the lines in a great painting. They seem to contradict everything I have already written. I have said that my theory of life is that of Behavior as Games, but can what happened be called a Game? Has it not gone far beyond the games of the Count and Bonnie?

This was a question I faced in wretchedness and agony of spirit. I sought for the answer in the Master, in Friedrich Nietzsche. And I found it. Hear what Zarathustra says of the Pale Criminal:

One thing is the thought, another thing is the deed, and another thing is the idea of the deed. The wheel of causality doth not roll between them.

An idea made this pale man pale. Adequate was he for his deed when he did it, but the idea of it, he could not endure when it was done.

So far you might interpret that we may think things, yet must not do them, that the idea of the deed is permitted but not the deed itself. This is Behavior as Games. But it is wrong! For what the Master says in the end is that the purity of intention is what

70

matters. When the judge says: "Why did this criminal commit murder? He meant to rob," Zarathustra replies: "I tell you that his soul wanted blood, not booty. He thirsted for the happiness of the knife." The impulse was pure, the desire for the happiness of the knife. The Superman is lightning, is frenzy. "It is not your sin—it is your moderation that crieth unto heaven."

I am not a Superman, I am a poor weak feeble being. (As the Master was too.) Yet I have been part of Great Events, I have not been tamed into moderation.

Two Great Events, I say, but really only one. A Great Event should have a plan and a design, and the first occasion lacked both. It was crude, unfortunate, wrong. The girl expected sex, and Dracula and Bonnie—what was their intention? I have tried to understand, but remain unsure. Yes, I do know—they wanted it too. Then she became frightened, and Dracula was angry. Perhaps he was frightened also. We were all weak, all foolish.

I do not regret what happened. *The way* it happened I regret. If the Event was Great the humans were not equal to it.

I shall say no more about it.

But the Second Event was different. All planned, all perfect. The design of superiority.

Sitting in the darkness watching that film (a *Dracula*, made in 1958, too modern but with some exciting scenes—in one, Dracula's *eyes* are bloody), I considered the girl. I sat one row back from her, I could have touched her on the shoulder. But the time was not yet! I looked at the images chasing each other on the screen and I watched the head in front of me and I thought my thoughts.

Bonnie had told her that I would be there, and that she would meet me. Her curiosity had been roused. I could see that she was disappointed, bewildered, thought it all a fraud. Bonnie was waiting down the street and spoke to her, saying I'd been delayed. I got into my car and flashed the lights as I passed, the signal to say that everything was all right, we should go ahead.

Then I waited down the road and leaned out of the window as they were passing. Bonnie said, "Here he is," and half pushed her into the car—although not exactly pushed, for the girl was getting in quite willingly. I spoke to her, then drove off. All perfectly done.

She looked at me and then at Bonnie and I could see in the mirror that she was surprised and meant to ask questions, would say she wanted to get out perhaps. But she had no chance. Bonnie had the ether pad ready, and put it quickly over her face.

Bonnie has been wonderful, a true helpmate. Alone I would have been powerless; with her I can do anything. "I and me are always too earnestly in conversation: how could it be endured, if there were not a friend?" Bonnie is the friend I need. My inferior, but my friend.

Of the rest I do not bring myself to write. It was all glory and fulfillment, and as fulfillment must be, all blood and filth and horror. The agony is the test. In the midst of it I felt myself the controlling force, calm, supreme, superior, without pity. "Upward goeth our course from man on to superman."

And yet—can this be believed?—there was part of me that wished it had not been necessary, that it could have been different. Some things that Bonnie did repelled me.

Comments, Regrets, Thoughts. These were Great Events, especially the second. The greatest in my life. Yet in both the sexual element was present. It must be exorcised. What happens must be pure.

My chief regret is that the tape recorder was never used. We were too stirred, our feelings too vivid. Yet this again was human weakness. At the center of violence there must be a total calm.

Another regret. Leaving that carryall and purse on the bus. A foolish thing to do. Much better to have kept it or buried it.

Bonnie is my creature. She does what I tell her and in this finds her fulfillment. The Master said: "The happiness of man is 'I will.' The happiness of woman is 'He will.'"

I said that everything I had previously written is contradicted by these Events. Yet is it really so? The Count played with Bonnie to the limit of fantasy. Now that the fantasy has become real, is it any less a Game? I go about my daily affairs as I always did, nobody looks at me and says, "That man is different." I can say to every man: "I look like you, I am like you, I *am* you." Every man plays such Games as mine in his mind. To make them real, is not that the greatest Game of all?

So ends this June.

13

Planter's Place

▬▬▬▬▬▬▬▬▬▬▬▬▬▬▬▬▬

The girl's name was Hazel Palmer. She had known Louise well at school, and was now a secretary in an engineering office. She had been out with her boyfriend in his car on the night of June 20, and as they were driving along between Riverend and High Ashley they had noticed a car parked at the side of the road, and two people getting out. Both were women, and Hazel had noticed them first because one was staggering and the other was helping her. The staggering one leaned against the side of the car, and was clearly visible in the headlights as they passed. Hazel had recognized her as Louise. She had said to her friend Jack Jenkins that it was a school friend of hers, and that she was ill or drunk. Why hadn't they stopped? Well, the woman seemed to be looking after her, and Jack had his mind on other things. She thought the woman and Louise had both got out of the back doors, but couldn't be sure. If there was somebody else in the car she hadn't noticed. The car might have been an Austin, a Morris or a Ford, nothing unusual anyway. And she had no idea of the number.

And afterward? Afterward she and Jack had gone up to Brier Hill, a well-known place for loving couples, and had come home a different way. Then on Tuesday morning she had gone on holiday, and had been away all week. When she returned she

74

learned what had happened, and got in touch with the police.

Hazel Palmer did not seem very intelligent, but she stuck to her story through some skeptical questioning by Hazleton. What was the girl wearing? A dress with a miniskirt, but in the darkness she couldn't be sure of the color. What made her so sure it was Louise, when she could have seen her for only a few seconds? She just was sure, that's all. Could she say where it was that they saw her? She thought so. They were trying to find the place now.

Riverend was a small village just off the main road. Out of the village one road led back to the coast road, the other climbed up into the downs to High Ashley. This was southern England, an unmenacing countryside, the downs no more than gentle hills. Yet it was a lonely road for such a populous area. If you stopped in the right place, a shriek or two would almost certainly not be heard.

Hazleton looked sideways at the girl, who sat between him and Plender. She's enjoying it, he thought, having the time of her life. Hazleton did not much care for the young. He had two teen-agers of his own, and he simply did not understand their attitude to life, or the things that gave them pleasure. If this little bitch is wasting our time I'll have a few things to say to her, he thought savagely.

She was looking out of the window now, and chewing her lip. "Can you ask the man to slow down? I think we're getting near." The detective constable in front heard, and slowed to ten miles an hour. They were traveling on the level, with green fields on either side. After a couple of hundred yards she shook her head. "This isn't it." She turned to Hazleton, sensing his distrust. "It's not easy, you know."

Plender smiled at her. "We know that. Just tell us when you seem to recognize anything."

They went on for another half mile and passed a crossroads. "Now," she said. "Slow down, please. It was a bit after that." A quarter of a mile further on she said, "Here. Before that bend in the road ahead. I remember I was looking back and we went round the bend."

They all got out of the car. It was a hot day. Hedgerows ran along both sides of the road, wild flowers of some kind scented the air. There were no marks of a car having stopped. They pushed around in the hedgerows without result. Then the constable, who had gone ahead, called, "Sir."

They came up to him. Through a gap in the hedge there was a grassy path. At the end of it, a hundred yards back from the road, stood a stone cottage with tiled roof. The upstairs windows were broken, paint had peeled from the front door. Hazleton picked up a signboard that had fallen into the hedge. It said in faded letters: *Planter's Place.*

Hazleton and Plender looked at each other. "Edwards," Hazleton said. "Just take Miss Palmer back to the car while we have a look."

They made their way in silence through what had once been a garden. A few flowers struggled among the weeds. The front door did not give to the hand and they walked around trying windows and looking inside at empty rooms. On the way they passed an outhouse and a water butt. At the back a small window was two or three inches open. Plender looked at it speculatively. They walked around the rest of the house. There was a locked back door. One window was boarded up, the others shut tight. Hazleton nodded, came back and examined the small opened window. A layer of unsmeared dirt showed on it. "All right, what are you waiting for?"

Plender got his fingers inside and pushed. The window creaked open. He put head and shoulders in, then disappeared. There was a crash. His voice came from inside. "Landed on some old crockery. Sort of scullery. What shall I open, back door or front?"

"Neither. One of those other windows. Keep the doors for prints."

Plender opened a side window and watched with some awe

as Hazleton's bulky body came through. There was a sound of splintering as part of the windowsill came away with him. The DCI picked at the wood with a nail, and it flaked off. "Dry rot."

They were in what had obviously been a sitting room. The fireplace was modern, the flowered wallpaper torn. There was no furniture. Hazleton sniffed. "Somebody's been here. Smell it?" Plender could smell nothing. "And they didn't come in by any of the windows. Nor did they break in the door. There's an obvious conclusion, eh, Harry?"

"Yes, sir."

The front door was on a spring lock, the back door bolted. In the back room flakes of pastry, possibly bits from a pie, were on the drain board. They looked recent.

"Our old friend the passing tramp?" Plender suggested.

"How did he get in?" Hazleton's face, square and heavy-jowled, with the knobs on it gleaming, was somber. "I'll tell you something else I smell, Harry. Blood."

There were two bedrooms on the upper floor. In the back one the lower part of the wall was splattered with marks of a bright, recent red. Rust-colored stains were on the floorboards. On the boards, and on a kitchen chair, there was candle grease. He's certainly got a nose for it, Plender thought. In one corner of the room were some clothes—a pink dress that looked small enough for a child, briefs, brassiere, shoes. It occurred to Plender afterward as pathetic that they should have made such a tiny pile, but at the time he felt only a thrill of recognition. Hazleton prowled around the marks and then said in a harsh voice, "Come on, then. Let's find her."

They unbolted the back door. The sky was still blue, the sun shone, but to Plender there was now something sickly in the country smell; it seemed to him that the scent of blood was mingled with that of the long grass and the flowers. It was he who opened the door of the outhouse. He saw rusty buckets, an old coalbin on its side, some bits of corrugated iron. He moved further in, among empty tins, some old sacks, and lifted these to uncover what looked for a moment like a paler sack beneath. But only for a moment. He went out again and called Hazleton.

The big man went into the outhouse and came out again. He looked at Plender. "Pull yourself together. You've seen a dead girl before, haven't you? They look worse after traffic accidents."

"Yes, sir."

"I want you to drive us back. Edwards can stay here."

Hazel Palmer sat in a corner of the car, temporarily forgotten. She looked at them and said, "You've found Louise."

"You were right to come to us. She's dead." Hazleton got in beside her, patted her hand and sighed. "I wish you'd read the papers while you were on holiday."

14

Ends, Mostly Dead

━━ ━━ ━━ ━━ ━━ ━━ ━━ ━━ ━━ ━━ ━━ ━━ ━━ ━━ ━━ ━━

If one is horrified by medical detail, then the report on Louise Allbright was fairly horrifying as such things go. The cause of death was strangulation by some kind of ligature, but when this occurred she must have been in an enfeebled state, for some four dozen incisions had been made in her body, so that by the time she died she must have been a mass of blood. Most of the cuts were trivial, but some had been on her nipples and in the vagina, as well as under her armpits and on her face and neck. The incisions had been made with some sharp thin instrument like a razor blade. There were severe bite marks on her neck. When she was found her hands were tied behind her back with electric light cord. There had been no sexual connection, but a sexual assault had taken place in the form of an attempt to force some object up her vagina. Louise Allbright had not been a virgin.

So far the medical details, which did not horrify any of the policemen who read them. They were not of much direct help in giving a line to her murderer, nor was Dr. Otterley, the pathologist, able to say whether more persons than one had been involved. Some of the cuts were deeper than others, so that the light ones might have been made by one hand and the deep ones by another, but this was frankly conjecture. Nor were the fingerprint details of much help. There were a number in the room with bloodstains on the walls where she had presumably been tortured and killed, but most of them were blurred and some were her own. The front door, about which Hazleton had been so careful, yielded only a number of blurred impressions. There were some prints on the outhouse door, but it was quite likely that they were not connected with the case.

The discovery of the body, and the nature of the injuries, however, brought full-scale attention in the press. There were pictures of what was called the murder cottage, and a heightened account of what Hazel Palmer had seen, under the heading WHO WAS THE MYSTERY WOMAN? All known local sexual deviants were interrogated. Few of them had any record of sadistic violence but they were still interrogated, without result.

The existence of an actual body, as distinct from a theoretical suspicion about foul play, changed the police pecking order. A murder case outside a big city is normally in the charge of the head of the County CID, and when the body was found Paling took over a job for which he was not by nature well suited. Paling was aware of his own limitations. He knew himself to be a skeptic, lacking in the positive aggressiveness that makes a really good detective. He soon got bored with interrogating suspects, found many of them distressingly uncouth, and regarded most of the uniformed or plainclothes policemen he knew as only one or two degrees nearer civilization.

Paling was a bachelor who lived in an expensive service flat. He subscribed to the *Numismatist* and was deeply interested in collecting old coins. He never went to police concerts or dances, and was known at County HQ as the Toff. Such were his disadvantages. On the other hand, Paling had the ability to administer and coordinate that many good detectives lack. He took on this role in the Allbright case, giving Hazleton control of day-to-day inquiries. The DCI had the feeling that he was somehow being cheated by a man more sophisticated than himself. Why was it always Paling who made statements to the press? Hurley received another rocket for his slackness, and had no further connection with the case. Hazleton had, however, formed a good opinion of Plender, and gave him a good deal to do. It was Plender who conducted an interview which proved vital to the case when he saw Mr. Borrowdale, of Borrowdale and Trapney, at his office in Broad Street, just off the High Street.

Hazleton's obvious conclusion from the fact that the windows of the cottage were closed and the doors not broken in was that entrance had been made with a key. A key meant the estate agents, and they were Borrowdale and Trapney. They were the oldest-established agents in Rawley, but the flyblown pictures in their offices, the threadbare carpet and the general air of gloom made it clear that they were not the most successful.

Success, indeed, seemed an alien word in the presence of Mr. Borrowdale. He was a lank man in his sixties with large hands that had reddish knuckles the size of walnuts, which cracked occasionally, and a few strands of black hair plastered over an otherwise bald yellow head. His laborious voice was that of a preacher who has long since lost most of his congregation.

"Yes, Planter's Place is ours," he acknowledged. The idea obviously did not cheer him. He went to a filing cabinet, took out a sheet of paper and handed it to Plender, who saw that it contained the typed details of the property, beginning: "A DE-LIGHTFUL COUNTRY COTTAGE in need of some renovation." He put the paper in his pocket. "It's been with us for, oh, a couple of years now. It was owned by a man named Medina who had been a tea planter in Ceylon and then came home. He wanted a place of his own, and named it accordingly. A humorous name, you see. But it wasn't his for long, poor fellow. He died five years ago, and it's been empty ever since. Has dry rot, you understand." He lowered his voice as if he were referring to bad breath. "It may be that this unhappy affair will stimulate some interest. People do like a house where there has been a murder.

But there would still be the dry rot. Selling houses today, Mr. Plender, is not easy."

Plender was momentarily diverted. "I understood prices were going up all the time."

Mr. Borrowdale cracked his knuckles. "So they are. But all the business here goes to these newfangled agents, the ones who produce advertisements saying that a place is falling down and is very ugly, and yet manage to make it sound a bargain. Gammon of Gammon and Moody is very strong on that. He and Pilbeam get all the new business that's worth anything. Do you know Pilbeam? I understand he's a very go-ahead man."

He showed every sign of being able to continue for a long time in this vein. Plender broke in. "I'd just like to get straight about your procedure in letting people look at empty houses. Do you go round with them?"

"Sometimes. When it seems justified. In the case of Planter's Place I fear that wouldn't be the case."

"You take a note of their names and addresses, give them the keys and let them go out alone."

There was a rusty noise like a crow's caw which Plender did not identify for a moment. It was Mr. Borrowdale laughing. He wiped his eyes with a large, not very clean handkerchief. "In theory that would be the procedure."

"But not in practice?"

"In practice junior staff is junior staff, idle and inefficient. That has been my experience in recent years. I daresay Gammon may get some bright young fellows, but even Gammon was telling me when I met him at the yearly conference—"

It was clearly necessary to cut Mr. Borrowdale short. "Do you mean you've got no list of the people who were given an order to view?"

"I have a list." He handed it across the table and Plender saw that there were ten names on it. "But it is far from complete. People have come in, they have been given the key, no note has been taken of their names. I fear that often happens."

"You would have no record of them at all?"

"I fear not." Mr. Borrowdale paused, cracked his knuckles, decided to confide still worse news. "In some cases keys are not returned."

"I see."

"We make allowances for that." A wan smile said that estate agents, Gammon and Pilbeam apart perhaps, needed to make allowance for every sort of human frailty. "We always keep one extra set of keys for every property. Then if a set is not returned we have another one made. Our bill over the year for new keys would surprise you."

"Do you know whether anybody kept the keys for Planter's Place?"

"By the law of averages I should say it would be two or three people each year." Another wan smile appeared, like weak sun breaking through cloud. "But we know, don't we, that the law of averages doesn't always work."

That was the effective end of an interview which left Plender feeling rather low-spirited. The names on the list were checked out, and none of the people appeared to have any conceivable connection with the case. There this line of approach finished, in an end apparently dead. When the whole thing was over, however, Plender realized that there was a question he might and perhaps should have asked, a question that arose from what had been said. If he had asked the question, would the answer have made any difference? He was never able to make up his mind. But nobody else commented on his omission, and like a wise man Plender never mentioned it.

It was Plender also who talked again to Ray Gordon. The journalist's movements on that Monday evening had involved going from one place to another in search of a story, and they had proved almost impossible to check in detail. It was not this, however, so much as the nature of his relations with Louise that interested the police.

"Look, I've told you, I didn't have any relations. I said that when I first spoke to you."

"You didn't say then that she'd been passed on to you by the Lowson girl. I still don't see quite how that could happen."

"I took Sally Lowson out a few times. She was a good dancer and she's quite a piece, if you like big girls. Then, I don't know, she seemed to go off me." His neat face screwed up into displeasure at the idea. "One night she just said, 'We've had it,' and that was that. I suppose a journalist on a local paper wasn't interesting enough for her. Snobbish bitch."

"And how did Louise come into it?"

"Then she said, 'I'll tell you a girl who's really got hot pants for you, Louise Allbright. You should do something about her sometime.' So I took her out a couple of times. Three, actually."

"But she hadn't."

"Hadn't what?"

"Hot pants for you. You said you didn't make her."

"I told you what she was like, that she wanted excitement but was too timid to go out and get it. She was the sort who'd settle down in the end with a man twice her age and then complain about having a dull life."

Plender also went around one evening and had a chat with Paul Vane about the incident at the tennis club. Vane, a tall, handsome but rather nervous man, laughed at the idea that it might have rankled with Gordon. What sort of girl was Louise? Plender asked.

"I've no idea; I hardly knew her." Vane was looking at a spot behind Plender. He turned and saw that Mrs. Vane had come into the room. "She seemed pleasant enough. Very young."

"My husband takes a kindly interest in young girls," Alice Vane said from behind Plender.

"Alice, for God's sake." She walked out of the room. "Another beer, Sergeant?"

"Thank you, sir, very nice of you."

Vane poured whisky for himself and splashed soda on the

tray. "My wife's nervy. She hasn't adjusted yet to life down here. It's nonsense, what she was saying."

"About your kindly interest in young girls, sir?"

"Yes. I mean, it *is* a kindly interest, if you want to use that phrase; nothing more."

"To go back to that bit of bother at the tennis club—"

"It was really absolutely nothing."

"You took Louise Allbright home afterward."

"Yes, I believe I did. Why?"

"You're employed by Timbals Plastics in London, is that right?"

"I'm their personnel director. Why?"

"Louise's father is with them too, only he's here in Rawley." Plender pretended to look at his notes. He remembered perfectly what Mrs. Allbright had said, and now repeated it. "His wife said one of the bosses at Timbals brought her home that night and wanted to make love to her, but she wouldn't let him."

Plender was surprised by Vane's reaction to what was really not much more than a routine inquiry. He actually flinched away, as the sergeant put it to Hazleton later, as if you'd stuck a branding iron in front of his nose. The struggle for self-control lasted only a few seconds. Then Vane was himself again, a man rather too eagerly friendly.

"That's preposterous."

"You mean it's not true?"

"After what you call the bit of bother—and believe me, even to call it that is to exaggerate it out of all proportion—we stayed there talking and playing darts. Then I drove her home and kissed her good night. Nothing more."

"It's not true that you tried to make love to her and she wouldn't let you?"

"Absolute rubbish. Who did she say this to?"

"Her parents."

"I should say she was showing off. Trying to impress her father because he works at Timbals."

"Yes, sir." Plender had become perceptibly more formal in the course of the conversation. "As a matter of form, could you tell me where you were on the evening of June twentieth?"

"I expect so." He looked at a pocket diary. "A fairly ordinary day. I caught the six-something home, was back here just before seven-thirty. Then I stayed in the rest of the evening, had dinner, watched TV."

"Just stayed in with your wife? Nobody called, no telephone calls, you didn't go out?"

"No." Vane smiled, at ease now. "I've just remembered. We had a cold meal, which Alice had made in advance because she felt a migraine coming on. She's taken to playing a lot of bridge, and I believe the concentration on it is bad for her. She ate nothing, went to bed around nine o'clock. Later I worked on some papers I'd brought home from the office."

"I believe your daughter lives here?"

"Yes. But she was out till midnight. She's moved out altogether now, taken a flat in London with friends. The younger generation, you know."

Plender left it at that. There was nothing against Vane really, nothing beyond his wife's hostility and his own embarrassment on the subject of young girls. They ran a check with CRO, but he had never been charged with any offense.

Hazleton himself talked to Sally Lowson, feeling that this was appropriate in dealing with the daughter of a friend of the chief constable. He had a whisky and a bit of a chat first, and was impressed by the wall panel and the drinks tray. He was impressed too by Sally, who seemed to him a fine figure of a young woman. When he was left along with her he smelled something. Sex? Fear? A mixture of both perhaps, but anyway something that he found exciting. If I wasn't a married man with a couple of kids, and if I were a few years younger, I'd take this girl out and I bet before the evening ended I'd have screwed her, he thought.

He already had Plender's report on Gordon's statement. Sally put things a little differently when he asked about it.

"I did go around with him a bit, but it was a dead loss. I mean, he talked about nothing but himself and his work all the time. After the second hour I stopped listening." Her smile showed fine large teeth.

"So you packed him up. Did you suggest to him that Louise Allbright was interested in him?"

"I think I did say something like that. Louise thought he was good-looking. So he is, if you like little men."

But you like big men, my beauty, Hazleton thought. "She went out with him, as you know. Did she say anything to you about that? Putting it bluntly, Miss Lowson, did she say whether she'd had intercourse with him? I'm sorry if the question embarrasses you, but what she said might be important."

"It doesn't embarrass me at all. The answer is no. I mean, she didn't tell me, but I very much doubt it."

"Did she mention any other affairs?"

"She told me she'd been to bed with a boy two or three times. At some pop festival last year. All she said about Ray was that she'd had a good time—that was the first time she went out with him. Afterward she didn't seem so keen. Perhaps he'd given her his lecture on journalism." Hazleton sensed an evasiveness in her response, especially when she went on talking. "I didn't know her that well, just through the tennis club. I felt a bit sorry for her, really. I mean, she obviously wanted to have a man of her own, but she was nervous of going out to get one. You know she went to Keep Fit classes?"

"Yes. It's been suggested that she'd have been more likely to go for an older man. Would you think that was so?"

"I've no idea."

"As far as you know, she didn't go out at all with a man of that sort?"

"No." For some reason the question seemed to make her nervous. When he probed round and round about it, though, like a dentist looking for a nerve end, he got no further response.

Neither Hazleton, Plender, nor anybody else working on the case got any further in discovering hidden depths in Louise Allbright. Her school friends said she was the quiet type, her mother and father that she had always been a good daughter who never gave them a minute's trouble—the Isle of Wight escapade now forgotten. The carryall had obviously been put in the London bus in an attempt to divert attention from Rawley, and if Hazel Palmer had not been passing by Planter's Place it might have achieved that object, since the body might well not have been found for weeks. There was no clue to the meaning of the envelope fragment with a number on the back.

The sum total of discovery from these investigations was not great. Beyond the fact that her murderer owned or had access to a car there was no clue to his identity. Indeed, the assumption that he was male was not justified, nor was the use of the singular. It seemed likely that two people were involved, and they might be two women, or a man and woman. It seemed almost certain that this was a murder without a rational motive, prompted by sadism.

"And we know what a problem that kind of thing can be," Hazleton said gloomily to Paling. "People just don't seem to notice anything connected with sex and crime. Remember that girl who was raped and killed and then dumped? Three boys saw a man take her body out of a car and put it in the bushes, five other people saw him too, and still nobody tried to stop him or do anything about it."

"Cheer up. These are the dog days. Here's something interesting. You remember Anne Marie Dupont?"

"The French girl? Of course."

"I wrote to her family—you remember they collected her

things without our having a look at them? What was the name of that inspector who thought they were of no interest? Hurley, yes, I'll remember that. Anyway, I've had a letter from the sister with which I needn't bother you—it's in French."

Supercilious bastard, Hazleton thought. Paling was known to regard himself as a French scholar.

"She repeats that although her sister was interested in men (she doesn't put it in quite that way) she wouldn't have gone off for good without telling her family. But she found this letter among her sister's things."

He pushed a photostat across the table. The letter was typewritten, with no address at the top.

My dear Anne Marie

Thank you for the photograph. May I keep it? It is in front of me now as I write, and I think you look wonderful. So appealingly fresh and gay, and with that certain look in your eye which says you are French and not English.

And now, shall we meet? I hope so. I look forward to introducing you to the group. We are prepared to discuss anything and everything, as I told you. Nothing is barred! You ask about women members. Yes, there is one in particular. I want you to meet her. Can you be at the corner of Boundary Road at 6 o'clock on Friday evening? I'll pick you up from there. Sorry I can't ask you to come to the place where we meet, but there are reasons. I hope you can manage this, and look forward to seeing you.

Sincerely
Abel

"Boundary Road," Hazleton said. "Near Rawley station. And I'll tell you another thing. There aren't many houses there; it's all warehouses and factories. And Friday, May twenty-seventh, was the day she disappeared."

"The lab have given us a report on the machine that typed this. It was an Olivetti portable between five and ten years old, letters *a* and *e* rather worn, *c*, *t* and *l* slightly out of alignment.

Thousands of them about, unfortunately. What else do you get from the letter?"

"They haven't met, so how did they get in touch? One of those friendship circles? The sort of thing where you put in an ad: 'Gentleman in thirties, attractive, well-to-do, interested music and the arts, would like to meet attractive younger lady. . . .' "

"You've got the tone. And this was just the sort of girl who'd answer an advertisement like that, telling herself it was a joke but being a bit serious about it too."

"What about Louise Allbright? Isn't she the sort of girl who'd have answered that kind of ad too? I think we may be on to something."

Paling, who had already reached this conclusion, now applauded it. "What about the writer? Forty or round about, wouldn't you say from the phrasing? 'That certain look in your eye' and 'We are prepared to discuss anything and everything.' No young man would write like that."

"Married. Or single with a landlady, but more likely married. That's why he can't ask her to the place where they meet. Lives in Rawley."

"Or works here, lives outside. What about his occupation?"

"Not a manual worker. Some sort of professional job, I'd say. Not an important one, too fussy and pedantic. Civil servant perhaps, assistant accountant who won't get any higher, chief clerk, likes to think himself the pillar of the firm but will get the sack one day, that kind of thing. And I should say he's probably nearer fifty than forty."

"Anything else strike you?"

"The name, you mean?" Paling nodded. "No, I don't make anything of that. Except that it won't be Abel."

"Would you say he might have had a religious upbringing? I don't mean he's a clergyman, but very likely a regular church-goer, sidesman, choirmaster, something like that. Too far-fetched? Perhaps you're right." Paling gave a delicate little laugh. "We don't want to sound too much like Sherlock and Mycroft, do we?"

Hazleton, who had never read the Sherlock Holmes stories, ignored this. "If the two cases are linked—and we still don't know for certain that they are, though it looks like it—then Louise belonged to this friendship circle too. That number on the envelope is presumably something to do with it. And if Louise had joined one of these clubs or circles she must have left some record of it."

"And if you find a choirmaster mixed up in it, we're home and dry."

Hazleton left thinking that the Toff wasn't so stuffy after all. But the prospects that looked so promising came to nothing. The Services knew nothing about Anne Marie's private affairs, and a letter sent by Paling to the sister in France brought a negative reply. A meticulous check on all Louise's correspondence—which didn't take long, because there was so little of it —revealed nothing connected with any friendship organization. Since Louise had always been down to collect the post in the morning her parents did not know whether she had been receiving letters recently, but she had never mentioned such a thing to them as they felt sure she would have done. Allbright seemed to think that the whole thing was an oblique way of suggesting that his daughter was unpopular, and that this reflected on him. There were no friendship circles registered in or around Rawley, although this did not mean much since many of them were unregistered. The garden of Planter's Place was dug up in the hope of finding Anne Marie's body, and the nearby fields searched, without result. The characteristics of the Olivetti on which the letter had been typed were circulated, in case it should have come into a dealer's hands, again without result. Progress on the case came to a dead stop.

15

Personality of a Murderer

━━ ━━ ━━ ━━ ━━ ━━ ━━ ━━ ━━ ━━ ━━ ━━ ━━ ━━

The Vanes had at last asked the Lowsons to dinner, and the Services too. Alice had spent the afternoon at the bridge club, where she and Mrs. Clancy Turnbull had won rubber after rubber, and she arrived home in too exhilarated a state to pay much attention to the cooking. It was not a comfortable meal. The first course was some kind of fruit concoction in jelly, and the jelly had not set properly. The boeuf stroganoff that followed was as tough as leather, and in some mysterious way the sour cream in the sauce appeared to have curdled. The cheese, however, was impeccable. Now they sat out in the garden on a fine July evening, drinking coffee and brandy. It was Penelope who mentioned the Allbright case, saying that the police now seemed to think it was linked to the disappearance of their au pair.

"I mean, they go on and *on*, asking all sorts of really personal questions about her which I absolutely . . . can't answer. I can only keep on repeating that she was a silly little thing. I mean, I'm terribly sorry if something's happened to her, but I will *not* be made to . . . feel guilty."

"It's pretty horrible, what they did to the other girl," Valerie Lowson said. "From what I hear she was pretty well cut to ribbons. We had the police round too. Sally knew the girl slightly. You knew her too, Paul, didn't you?"

"Oh yes, indeed. 'What were your movements on the night in question?' And all I'd done was play tennis with her." Paul, who wore a blazer with brass buttons and very tight dark trousers, needed only a peaked white cap to look like a member of a yachting club.

"Cut to ribbons." Valerie drank a little of her coffee, and shuddered. "What kind of person could do a thing like that?"

Dick Service had been working on his pipe. Now it puffed away like a tiny steam engine. "Inadequacy. That's the mark of sex criminals."

Bob Lowson held up his hand. "Silence for the company psychologist. You mean the police ought to be looking for a henpecked man trying to assert himself? I thought it was poisoners who did that."

"And other sex criminals. Well, most criminals if it comes to that. They're overcompensating for some inadequacy in their personal lives. Often it's got social origins; they have the feeling that other people look down on them because of their birth or their limp or their bad breath or something. Sometimes it's a straight sexual inadequacy, which can be prompted by anything —a single incident of rejection, the loss of a lover to a rival who's younger and more attractive—"

"Impotence?" Alice was sitting near the French doors leading into the house, her face in shadow. She had said little during dinner. Now she spoke the word with emphasis.

Dick took out his pipe, put it back again. "Impotence? Yes, of course."

Valerie leaned forward. The lamplight illuminated the gap between her formidable breasts. "I thought the psychologists believed that all these things go back to childhood."

Given this golden opportunity, Dick dropped readily into the manner of the professor that he might have been if he had not settled for commerce and cash. "Perfectly correct. Everything goes back to childhood. In the life pattern of every serious criminal you will find some childhood disturbance. The most obvious is a broken home, furiously quarreling parents, one child treated quite differently from the rest. But there are lots of other possibilities, like a financial crisis changing the whole pattern of life, a child's separation from somebody he's loved intensely, some traumatic incident at school with a master or a fellow pupil. Anything that causes insecurity is a breeding ground for crime."

Bob Lowson held out his glass for another brandy. He had drunk just enough to be genially bellicose, and to be prepared to underline the fact that Dick was, after all, the company psychologist and nothing more. "Don't we all have things of that sort in our lives? I mean, look at me. I had an Irish nurse up to the time I was seven and I can't tell you the things she used to make me do." His laugh boomed out. "But it doesn't seem to have done me much harm."

"That would fit you, Paul," Alice said. She explained. "Paul's mother ran away with a commercial traveler when he was five. Then his father cleared off and he was brought up by two aunts. They used to beat him when he was naughty; wouldn't that be traumatic?"

"Did they beat you, Paul?" Bob said. "Did they now?" Paul did not reply.

It is natural to suppose that psychologists are more perceptive than other people of nuances in speech, but in fact many of them are startlingly impervious to any feelings except their own. So now, although Valerie looked hard at her husband, who gazed blandly back at her, and Penelope Service shifted in her chair, Dick seemed oblivious of anything uncomfortable in the scene. "Of course we're all to some extent insecure. It's the price we pay for being part of a highly complicated civilization. The whole form of this civilization—crimes, trials, prison sentences—makes us classify some people as criminals, bad elements in society, others as good elements. Essentially this is wrong. The 'bad elements' are the one on whom the greatest pressures have been applied, that's all."

Bob Lowson's waistband was tight, there was a bulge at his

crotch as his body sprawled in the armchair. "How do you know what pressures are applied to anybody, or how they adjust to them? How do you know, eh, Dick?"

This time the hectoring tone got through to Dick Service. He shrugged and was silent. There was a skirring sound as Alice's chair moved and she went inside the house. Valerie said, "They seem to think from what I've read that two people were involved, a man and woman. That wouldn't quite fit in with your theories, surely?"

"My belief is—and I can't substantiate this in any way, I'll give you that—that this might be a case of folie à deux."

"And what's that when it's at home?" Paul's laugh sounded contrived, uneasy. "Do you know about this kind of thing, Penelope?"

"You'd be surprised, the kind of thing I . . . know about." Penelope rolled her eyes. "You'd never believe the things people do. Don't let Dick give you the horrors."

"Folie à deux is unusual, but not all that rare." Dick was not to be deflected. "It's a psychological condition in which two people whose behavior apart from each other is harmless, or within the limits of what we call normal, behave quite differently when they are together. Then they may commit various antisocial acts. Sometimes they may attack each other; more often their relationship acts as an incitement to criminal acts— arson, theft, murder. My own belief is that folie à deux was present to some degree in the Moors Murders. I don't believe Myra Hindley would ever have done anything of that kind unless she'd met Brady. Or there's the Cleft Chin case just after the war, when an American deserter met a striptease dancer in London. They both told lies to each other, saying they were gangsters. Then they behaved like gangsters. They ended up killing a taxi driver."

"I'm getting the horrors," Paul said.

Valerie waved him down.

"No, I'm interested. So what do you think they'd be like, these people?"

Dick ignored his wife's warning glance. "The man, about forty, some sort of early traumatic experience, personally rather timid. Some subordinate occupation, not likely to own a firm or be managing director of it. If he is, it's unsuccessful. Possibly married, may have children, unsatisfactory sexual relationship with wife. Very respectable, that's important. A pillar of society. The woman I don't see so clearly. I should say she's subordinate to him—these relationships are almost always based on some sort of master-servant feeling—and so it's hard to say what she's like. I'd need to know more about the facts."

"You ought to give the police the benefit of all this. I mean it, you really should. I'm sure our friend the chief constable would be interested." This time the sneer in Bob's voice was unmistakable. Dick Service colored. Penelope got up to go, and so did Valerie. There was a crash from inside.

Paul ran in and the others followed him. Alice was half kneeling in front of an open cupboard door, looking at her hand. Blood was dripping onto the carpet. On the floor was a water jug in fragments. Paul acted quickly and efficiently, getting antiseptic and bandage. Penelope helped Alice to a sofa, where she sat looking straight in front of her.

"I cut myself. I was looking for photographs to show you, then I knocked over the jug and cut myself."

Paul tied the bandage. "But we don't keep photographs in with the jugs and glasses, do we, love?" He said as an afterthought, "What photographs?"

They were on the floor. Dick picked them up. They showed two small boys with neatly brushed hair, wearing school uniforms. Behind them like sentinels stood two tall women, each with hands on the shoulders of one of the boys.

"The aunts?" Dick said.

"And Paul. And his brother. Enough to cause a trauma, don't you agree? I'm sorry, I'm perfectly all right now."

96

Ten minutes later they had all gone. Alice said, "I'm sorry about the dinner. It was stupid, inefficient. It won't happen again."

"It's not important." He put a hand on her arm and she jerked away.

"Don't touch me. I don't want you to touch me."

"You let me bandage your arm."

"That was different."

After they got home the Lowsons argued about whether or not Alice had tried to cut her wrists. "With a man like that for a husband she might do anything," Valerie said. "I tell you, Bob, there's something wrong with him. Did you hear the way she said 'Impotent'?"_

"He's under lots of stresses, I'll give you that. I'll have to do something about it if it goes on." He stared at Valerie's powerful arms. "You're looking very masterful tonight."

She looked at him and sighed. "Not *that* again." As they were going up the stairs she said, "You were pretty awful to Dick Service. He may be a boring man, but there was no need to go on like that."

"If I have behaved badly I must be punished," he said meekly.

"You were so pompous about that case, darling," Penelope said as they undressed for bed.

"Was I? People seemed to be interested."

"No, you really were . . . pompous. Didn't you see how Bob Lowson was getting at you?"

"He'd had too much to drink."

"You'll land yourself out of a job if you're not careful." She paused. "Do you suppose it was right, all that stuff you said? About—what do you call it?—folie à deux?"

"Quite possibly. Very likely. Why?"

"It struck me about Paul. There's something wrong with that marriage."

"So?"

"I wondered why the police asked him to account for his movements the night that girl was killed. I wondered what he was doing when Anne Marie went."

"You're talking rubbish, Pen."

"Poor Anne Marie. She wasn't much good, but she was rather . . . sweet. I don't like to think she might be . . . dead."

16

Problems of a Personnel Director

The letter had "Personal and Confidential" written in red ink on the top left-hand corner. The name and address were in blue ink. The writing was an old-fashioned copperplate hand. Hartford slit the envelope with his letter opener. He read the contents twice, the second time with a frown of concentration. Then he rang for Joy Lindley and questioned her for ten minutes. After she had left him he pursed his lips in a soundless whistle, a sure sign that he was feeling cheerful.

The meeting at which Esther Malendine's paper on Job Enrichment and Deliberate Method Change was discussed took place later that morning. Paul and Esther were both present at the early part of it. Esther was asked to clarify some points, and then Paul gave his views. He got up looking remarkably slim and elegant. Bob Lowson wished fleetingly that he could look like that when he put on a suit.

"I think this is a very interesting project." Paul looked around with his most winning smile. "I say that although I had nothing to do with getting it under way. It's really Mr. Hartford's pigeon. At the same time I must say I'm not convinced that we shall see improvements which will justify the organizational upturn that would be involved. When you come down to it, what the whole thing amounts to is increasing the chances for individuals to use their initiative, treating them as human beings and not as cogs in a machine. At Timbals I hope we do that already."

There was a murmur of agreement. Sir George Rose said, "Miss Malendine mentions specific points about the ways in which the adoption of DMC would improve our efficiency, and she gives the increased output figures we might expect. Do you think she's wrong?"

"I wouldn't go that far. The figures are purely conjectural, that's all." Sir George nodded encouragingly. "When we're considering something that involves the setting up of teams in every section of our work to teach people how to do their jobs —because that's what it amounts to—I should need to be thoroughly convinced that we were working inefficiently before I agreed to it. Nothing in this paper convinces me of that."

Somebody said, "Here, hear." Sir George asked, "What do you say to that, Miss Malendine?"

Sunlight glinted on the smoked glasses. It was warm in the board room, although there was supposed to be air-conditioning. "I don't think that's the right approach. It isn't a question of people being lazy or not doing their best. The point is that an entirely different method of approach will produce better results. With a job-centered approach, such as we and most other firms employ, the manager in control of any group runs it in an authoritarian way. He praises some people, punishes others. What my paper proposes is moving over gradually to an employee-centered approach."

"No group manager?"

"Yes, but he'll see his job as building an effective work unit. Then he gives the unit an objective and lets them get on with it. The objective will be one that means higher output than was previously produced. Given a good work unit it's achieved, not through working harder but by coordinating better. Everybody benefits, the firm and the workers." She took off her glasses, revealing innocent eyes, put them back. "Obviously this doesn't happen overnight. People have got to learn to accept responsibility. Managers and executives may need training courses—T groups, Jay Burns Lawrence courses, and so on."

"Mr. Vane?"

"It sounds nice. I have the feeling that a good deal of it's just words."

Up the board room table faces looked at him. Sir George a meditative sheep, bull Lowson with head half lowered in classic position for charging, mean squirrel Hartford, other faces of dogs, goats, broad-nostriled camels. Faces silently contemplative, faces frowning. Not a good thing to have said. Sir George asked if there were any further questions. Hartford, the words coming slow as water for a Pernod dripper:

"Do you have any personal knowledge of the way in which Deliberate Method Change operates?" Paul said no. "But you understand the ideas behind it, you've read some of the behavioral scientists?"

"A little." The right moment to smile again. "I've been too busy coping with the actual problems of my department to have much time for theory. The problems belong to here and now."

Lowson. The bull raised his head and spoke pacifically. "As I understand it you're not denying the possible value of this Job Enrichment paper."

He took the chance eagerly. "Certainly not. There are important ideas in it. The practical application at the moment is what worries me."

It was over. He and Esther took the lift down a floor, walked in silence back to their offices.

In relation to Job Enrichment, and indeed to most other matters, only the opinions of Sir George, Lowson and Hartford were of much importance. The rest would try to discern the feelings of the big fish, and then swim along with them. They waited now to hear how Brian Hartford expressed himself. Job Enrichment and DMC were, as Paul Vane had said, his pigeons. He tapped Esther's paper.

"Some of this could have been put more simply, but the figures speak for themselves. We should give it a trial." Somebody murmured that there was something in what Vane had said, people at Timbals were treated like human beings already. Hartford responded impatiently.

"Vane's comments showed a lack of understanding about the very basis of a scheme like this. We're suffering from having as personnel director a man who's wholly untrained in scientific method."

Lowson said with conspicuous mildness, "Paul's come up through the company. That's something we encourage. Do you have criticisms of his work?"

"I don't doubt his competence to deal with day-to-day staff problems. In relation to DMC and output improvement I don't think he's learned the alphabet."

Battle was joined. It continued for half an hour on a level of apparent good humor, with Sir George acting as impassive but soothing umpire. Everybody around the table knew that something was at stake more than the actual adoption of the scheme, that Vane was Lowson's man and that Brian Hartford had brought in Esther Malendine. At the end of the half hour it had been agreed that a pilot scheme should be tried at Rawley. Hartford had a last word.

"I think it might be helpful to Vane to go on a Jay Burns Lawrence course." Fully aware that nobody else knew what he was talking about, he continued. "The object is to get top managers to become more aware of their own potentialities and those of other people. They're put into certain situations, they react, and then they examine the reactions themselves."

"Something like an army selection board where the candidates comment on their own performance?" somebody said, and Hartford agreed.

He stayed behind when the meeting was over. "I got a letter in the post this morning that you ought to see." He produced the letter with "Personal and Confidential" on the envelope. Lowson read it.

"Who is this girl mentioned in it, Joy Lindley?"

"The assistant to my secretary, Miss Popkin. At the moment, that is. I'm having her moved to another department."

"Is that fair? She's done nothing wrong."

"Nothing wrong," Hartford repeated evenly. "A girl who knows everything that happens in my office starts an affair with our personnel director—a girl of nineteen—and you say there's nothing wrong. That seems to me an extraordinary view."

"Perhaps she was hoping for a little personal Job Enrichment."

"And that's a deplorable remark."

"Yes. I'm sorry. But, Brian, I do feel you're making a mountain out of a molehill. We don't know if what's said here is correct. It may be all nonsense."

"Precisely. I thought you'd want to speak to Vane yourself."

Lowson stroked his slight paunch, a gesture that he always found reassuring. "Assuming that what's said here is correct, what do you suggest?"

For the first time Hartford showed slight uncertainty. "It's most undesirable that a top executive should carry on an affair with a junior member of our female staff."

"They don't positively say an affair in this letter, just taking her out. I agree it's stupid. I'll speak to Paul. But what then?"

"If the other story is true, we ought to consider carefully whether Vane is at all suitable as personnel director."

"I see. Hence the whatever-it-is course. We send him on it, say he reacted badly, give him a silver handshake. Is that what's in your mind?"

"Something like that. I think his reactions on the course will be slow and inadequate anyway. But if that letter is correct, in my opinion he's highly unsuitable for the job he does."

"I hope you never want any charity, Brian."

"I should never expect it."

Lowson got up. He looked a big formidable man as he towered over Hartford. "I'm not going to have anybody forced out because of some damned self-righteous busybody. Paul's private life is his own affair."

"When it becomes scandalous it's our affair too, surely? You realize that this letter will have to be answered."

When he was alone Lowson read the letter again with growing irritation. Why on earth couldn't people be sensible? In England now you could do almost anything you liked, but why do it in your own back yard? He canceled an appointment with Dr. Winstanley, and at lunch ate an omelet and drank nothing at all. Later he asked Paul to come in.

He appeared, schoolboyishly handsome, elegant, slightly apologetic. "Sorry if I threw too much cold water on that idea this morning, Bob. What was the decision?"

"The decision? We're going to run a pilot work study group at the Rawley factory and see what happens."

"Fine," Paul said heartily. "Good idea."

"There's something else. Do you know a girl named Joy Lindley? In Brian Hartford's office."

Paul crossed one leg over the other knee, showing an area of smooth silk sock. "Yes, I do."

"Are you having an affair with her?"

The leg was uncrossed. Paul looked astonished but not alarmed. "Of course not. I took her out for a couple of drinks one evening, that's all."

"That was a stupid thing to do. Brian's having her shifted to another department." Lowson paused. "A girl of nineteen in our office, Paul, a junior junior, and you're taking her out for drinks."

"I'll tell you how it happened." He launched into the story of her mistake about the memo and then grinned. "I was just applying those principles in Esther's paper, all that stuff about encouraging the staff."

Lowson did not smile back. "Do you know a girl named Monica Fowler?" To his dismay he saw Paul flinch. "There's a letter here from her father. Her mother is the sister of Joy Lindley's father. When Joy started talking about you at home they recognized the name. The letter was sent to Brian Hartford."

Paul Vane had gone very pale. A tic appeared in his cheek. He put up his hand to it, then withdrew it.

"Is it true, what the man says in this letter? You'd better read it." He passed over the letter and said, with an awareness of the incongruousness in the remark, "I had no idea you were connected with a youth club."

"It seemed—I always got on well with young people—tried to help them." He looked up from the letter, and spoke with something like indignation. "A lot of this is rubbish. I never had sex with Monica."

Bob Lowson felt as though he were a piece of elastic being stretched, stretched. When would he break and explode in wrath? "Tell me how much they've got wrong. The girl was thirteen. She was good at basketball, played for the youth club team. You coached them. She told her parents you often kissed her, you were always feeling her, several times you exposed yourself, you asked her to feel your privates and she did because she was frightened."

"She was never frightened. She was ready for anything. And it was all exaggerated."

"She was thirteen. Didn't you know how dangerous it was?" A vague hopeless gesture. "Then there's all this sickening stuff about it being impossible to make reparation. How much did they take you for?"

"Two hundred." In a barely audible mutter he added, "When I'd paid it they wrote and told Alice anyway."

"Don't you see—" Lowson began again, then stopped. He found stupid behavior unbearable, and this was very stupid. Looking at Vane's head bent again over the letter, avoiding his gaze, another thought occurred to him. "This was four years ago. How many other times has it happened? With girls under age, I mean."

"Only once. Earlier. Her parents were very understanding."

"But it could happen again. Any time."

"No. I'm over it now. I resigned from the youth club. I don't have anything to do with them now, young girls." Eagerly he said, "I mean, Joy Lindley is nineteen."

The whole thing was ridiculous, pathetic. Lowson had a strong desire to laugh. "Look, Paul, very likely half the girls under fourteen today are on the pill. For all I know, this Monica was a young tart and her mother and father played you for a sucker. I don't care what you do or who you do it with. That's not the point. The point is that I'm not having the organization mixed up in a scandal if I can avoid it. I won't have Timbals put at risk because you can't keep your hands off young girls."

"It's not like that; you don't understand." With the tic beating in his cheek he asked, "What are you going to do?"

Lowson said that he would have to think about it, and later that day talked again to Brian Hartford. As he had expected, Hartford's reaction was to say that they would be better off without a personnel director who mucked about with young girls. Lowson found himself defending Paul, and wondering why he did so. There was no doubt that something about Paul's persona made a strong appeal to him. But Lowson was not an introspective man, and he solved problems like these by ignoring their emotional content and committing himself to some practical action. He saw that he would have to make concessions to Hartford. He agreed that Paul should be sent on a Jay Burns Lawrence course, whatever that was. His future would depend on the report they received. From the gleam in Hartford's eye it was apparent that he had little doubt what sort of report it would be, but if this meant offering Paul up as a sacrificial lamb, Bob Lowson felt that he had deserved nothing better. In the meantime he wrote a brusque letter to Mr. Fowler, saying that the firm knew of this incident in the past, and that they were quite satisfied that Mr. Vane's relationship with Miss Lindley was purely a friendly one.

Sally Lowson spent the evening in Pamela's tiny flat near King's Cross. The flat was dingy, but according to Pam King's Cross was going to be the next fashionable district. Sally had been jittery ever since her interview with the police. Now she talked about going to them and telling them everything she knew.

"Do what you want, but that's plain stupid." Pam turned from the salad she was tossing. "What will you say? You know Louise wrote a letter to some man, you don't know if he replied. You'll be in the doghouse with everybody, and for what? I've got a better idea. I'll write to him myself." Over their cold chicken and salad she elaborated. "This man wrote to me, right? And we decided he seemed like a creep and didn't go on with it."

"Have you still got the letter?"

"Tore it up," Pam said through a mouthful of salad. "Why don't I write to him again, say I'm sorry I didn't answer before, say let's meet. Then we go along together."

"And what happens after that?"

"If he's sexy, sweetie pie, we have fun. And if he's old, you know, sixty or seventy, that might be fun too. I've often wondered what it would be like with a really old man."

"But supposing he's the man who—"

"Why, of course, sweetie, what we do quite early on is to drop in some phrase like 'I think you know my friend Louise Allbright' and watch his face. If we think he's been mixed up in something nasty we tell the fuzz."

"Pam, I don't know. I keep thinking about her."

Pam cleared away the plates. "Don't be soppy. You said what a boring girl she was, and I never met her so you can't expect me to cry my eyes out."

"Suppose something goes wrong."

"We'll meet him together; what can go wrong? Twenty to one he had nothing to do with it, but anyway we say, 'You are Colonel Plum and you committed the murder with a hatchet in the dining room.' Come on, stop looking like a sick cow and help me clear this stuff away. Freddy and Adrian are coming round in half an hour."

Later Sally rang up and told her mother that she was spending the night with Pamela. Her family had met Pamela. She had been to a good school and her father was in the Foreign Office. Bob and Valerie rather approved of her. Freddy and Adrian stayed the night too. Adrian worked in a merchant bank, Freddy had just opened a new boutique. In the morning they all drank orange juice and black coffee and went to work. For Sally it was a foretaste of the kind of life she would lead if she moved in with Pam. At some point in the evening she had agreed enthusiastically that Pam should write the letter.

17

Story of a Typewriter

━ ━━ ━━ ━━ ━━ ━━ ━━ ━━ ━━ ━━ ━━ ━━ ━━ ━━ ━━ ━━

"We may have found the typewriter," Plender said. "Pawnbroker in Chelsea named Marks says the details we gave check with one he had in a week ago. Brought in by a young woman. He's got her name and address."

Hazleton grinned at him. "What are you waiting for? Get on your horse."

Sammy Marks was brisk, smart, obviously intelligent. He showed Plender a specimen of something he had typed on his Olivetti. The sergeant compared it with a photostat of the "Abel" letter, and it was obvious that they had been typed on the same machine.

"Just bless Jewish curiosity, Sergeant," the pawnbroker said when Plender congratulated him. "And the fact that I like to try out everything in my stock. So I test this one, and then I remember the police notice, and I think: Those letters out of alignment; aren't they the same? And they are. So I pick up the telephone."

Plender, who had met few Jews but always believed that they would try to put something over on you, expressed his gratitude again. "You said a young woman brought it in."

"Five days ago, right. Good-looking bird, very cool, just above

109

medium height, early or mid twenties, dark hair, no wedding ring, wearing a dark green trouser suit."

"You should have been a detective, Mr. Marks."

"I notice things, that's why I'm going to be rich one day. Now I'll tell you something else. She said it was a temporary embarrassment. That's what they all say, but with her it could be true."

"What did you give her?"

"More than I should have done. Five on the typer, twenty on this." He pushed across a ring with a single diamond flanked by two rubies. "But it's not a bad ring. If she doesn't come back I won't make a loss."

"Have you got her address?"

Marks pushed over the relevant page of his book. Plender saw *Peacock, 59 Overbury Court, Kensington, W 8,* and made a note. The pawnbroker leaned over the counter and smiled. "Ask me whether I think it's right."

Showing off, Plender thought. "Do you think it's right?"

"The name, no. The address, possibly. But don't expect too much."

"What makes you say that?"

"It's the kind of thing I know," Marks said simply. "You catch up with her, you'll find I'm right."

Plender put a hand on the machine. "I'll have to take charge of this. I'll give you a receipt."

The pawnbroker sighed. "Do your duty as a citizen, and what does it ever get you but trouble?"

Overbury Court was a slightly decayed block of flats near Holland Park Road. The lift was self-operating, and there was no porter. Walking along the corridor, with its identical gray painted doors each differently numbered, Plender, who had married six months earlier and had a semidetached modern house with a nice little bit of garden back and front, wondered how people could choose to live in this way. He rang the bell

110

of 59. The door opened to reveal a short plump girl with a mass of frizzy hair. She stared at him.

"Are you Miss Peacock?"

"No. I'm Bella." She began to shut the door.

"Just a minute. Does she live here?"

"No. What are you from, a debt-collecting agency?"

He showed his ID card. The girl did not seem impressed. She called back over her shoulder, "Hey, Jen, there's somebody asking for Miss Peacock. Is that the name of the girl who skipped?"

Another head appeared behind and above Bella's frizzy hair and Plender thought: That's the one. "He says he's the fuzz. Do we let him in or do we stand on our rights?"

The other girl nodded and moved back into the room. Plender followed, thinking she looked rather like his wife, who was very cool like this girl, and had the same sort of dark good looks. She said now, "Who did you want?"

"I'm looking for Miss Peacock. She pawned a diamond ring and a portable typewriter recently."

Bella's mouth dropped slightly open. "Hey, Jen, that's—"

"It was you, wasn't it, miss? The pawnbroker described you."

"That's right," she said calmly. "It's the first time I've pawned anything, and somehow I didn't want my name on his ticket. You'd better sit down." She cleared papers off one armchair and sat in another herself. "What's it all about?"

"Routine inquiries. Your name's not Peacock, is it?"

"It's Vane. Jennifer Vane."

The name dropped into place, like tumblers in the lock of a safe. Vane, the man who had seen Louise home one night, and who got a bit flustered when it was suggested that he liked young girls. He had a daughter, or was it a stepdaughter? This would be the girl. Could she be the one who had met Louise after that film show? It seemed hard to believe, but Plender had known more improbable things to be true. He decided not to mention Rawley at present.

"Why did you put those things in pawn, Miss Vane?"

It was the frizzy-haired girl who answered. "Because she wanted the bread, why d'you think?"

Jennifer said, "Let's have a cup of coffee. Bella, love, you make it, will you?" When the other girl was out of the room, she said, "I don't know your name—"

"Plender."

"—but what's up, Mr. Plender? I put those things in hock because we've just moved in here, and it turns out that the girl we took the place from skipped owing a month's rent and leaving some bills unpaid. That's why Bella thought you were a debt collector."

"And the money for these things helped to pay the back rent?" Plender smiled. "I've been hard up myself, I can believe it."

"Right. Even at that it's a cheap flat, and cheap flats in London are like gold dust. I'll get the things back when our cash position's a bit less dicey."

Plender did not reply or comment. He was imagining what she would be like in bed. Would she be better than Gloria? It would be like having Gloria, except that this girl was somehow totally different from his wife while being strikingly similar. He was diverted from these thoughts by Bella, who came in and dumped down three cups of coffee. "Am I supposed not to be here? Or am I your partner in crime?"

"Stay by all means," he said. "The inquiry's about the typewriter. It may have some connection with an investigation."

"The *typewriter?*" Jennifer Vane's eyes opened wide. Her appearance of incredulity was convincing. "That's impossible. I mean, I brought it from home. It's my father's, though I've often used it too. We've had it for ages. I only moved out a few days ago, and I took it because I thought it might be useful."

"Did your family know you'd taken it?"

"Yes, of course. I don't understand. What's this all about?"

"I don't know too much about it myself. I've just been asked to make these inquiries, that's all. It came from up above, you know." He pointed to the ceiling and grinned. "Thanks very much anyway. Lovely coffee. By the way, can you let me have your parents' address?"

It was the one he knew, in Rawley.

Hazleton called round at Bay Trees on the following evening. Alice Vane opened the door, took him into the living room, where cards were spread out on the table, and called her husband. He came in wearing old trousers, dirty at the knees. He explained that he had been down in the cellar.

"Marvelous, the cellars in these old houses. Just fixing some wine racks to the walls for all the bottles we haven't got."

Hazleton considered him. Vane had hair rather longer than the DCI approved of, but he seemed an agreeable enough fellow, and looking at Alice's delicate profile bent over the cards he thought that she must have been a beauty in her time. Plender had said there was something odd about them, but to Hazleton they appeared a normal couple.

"Another grilling, Inspector? It was your sergeant last time. Are you prepared to drink with me? I believe that's always a good sign."

Hazleton accepted a whisky, and waited until it was in front of him. "It's about an Olivetti portable typewriter that was in your possession, sir. I should like to know where you got it and when, and where it is now."

"My little Olivetti." Many criminals are good actors—indeed, they tend to overreact rather in a ham actor's manner—and Vane's appearance of surprise meant nothing in itself. "But what on earth's that got to do with anything? Jen's got it now, hasn't she?"

His wife, bent over the cards, said, "Yes."

"We've seen Miss Vane. I understand she's had it only for the last few days. It's an earlier period we're interested in."

"Do you mind telling me why?"

The DCI said formally, "A letter we believe to have had a connection with the case was typed on that machine."

"On *my* machine?"

"There's no doubt about it. It was typed at some time before the twenty-seventh of May, probably a few days earlier."

"I don't know what to say. I mean, there isn't anything I can say. I bought the Olivetti about eight years ago, used it quite a bit at one time for typing reports and so on, not much lately. Then it was in storage. It moved here with us—no, come to think of it, a few weeks before us. It was in the stuff we had moved in here before we came in ourselves, isn't that so, love?"

"I believe so," Alice said, muffled.

"When we bought this house we had some trouble more or less at the last minute. The seller had a higher offer. That was after we'd moved in a bit of stuff because we thought everything was settled. In the end our agent persuaded him that he ought to take our offer."

"Tell me about it. And if you can do some checking of dates I'll be glad." The inventory from the storage firm showed that several items, including one portable typewriter, had been delivered to the house on the tenth of May. The Vanes had moved in on the first of June.

"It's very much like Planter's Place," Hazleton said to Paling. "For three weeks anybody could have been sent along by an estate agent, and they could have used the typewriter. Plender's talked to Darling, the agent who sold the house, and he says he didn't send anyone. That's reasonable, because he regarded the house as sold. But Darling's supposed to be a pretty fair stick-in-the-mud, and another agent called Gammon sent several people. He's a pretty bright character, Gammon. We've checked out all the people we can find, including one who made a higher offer to the seller, and they all seem harmless. But there are some we just don't know about."

"How about the seller—what's his name—Makepeace?"

"Over eighty and nearly blind. Nonstarter."

Paling put his fingertips together. "Doesn't all this strike you as highly improbable?"

"How d'you mean?"

"Here's our letter writer, looking for a machine on which he can type. He's also a potential home buyer. He happens to be looking round this house, spots the Olivetti, thinks: Ah hah, an ideal machine for me to use. And then—what? Is he going round alone, so that he sits down to type a letter on the spot? Or does he keep the key and come back later? Or does he take the machine away with him and bring it back again?"

"The man who made the offer came back three times. His name was Jamison. He's a computer engineer, came down to work in Rawley, bought another house now. Married, four kids. Trouble is he doesn't seem to have any connection with the case. He's got an alibi for the night Louise Allbright was killed."

"You see?"

"But *somebody* typed a letter on that machine."

"Precisely. So we're led to the conclusion that the person who typed the letter is the person who knew the machine was there, Vane himself. You say he's got no record?"

"None." Hazleton rubbed the knob of his chin. The sound was like a reaper cutting corn. "I don't know. He put on a good act, that's all I can say."

"So he puts on a good act. You've seen them before."

"But it was so dangerous for him." He stopped. Paling was shaking his white head.

"Not dangerous. He was unlucky. Why should anybody want to look at his typewriter? He types this letter, and no doubt some others too. Then his daughter says she'd like to have the machine. Marvelous, now it's out of the house. It's only the bad luck of her being hard up and pawning it, and then of the pawnbroker being so sharp, that's led us to him. I think you ought to put a man on him."

"Yes, sir."

"And get Sergeant Plender to look into his background a bit. Around the office, where he lived before, that kind of thing."

"Vane knows Plender."

"Never mind. Put a few shivers up his spine. I believe he's our man. It's a question of pinning it on him."

"Right, sir," Hazleton said, although he did not agree. He had not smelled anything wrong about Vane.

Pam sat at her desk and read the letter. It was neatly typed on a sheet of typing copy paper which had been folded over.

My dear Pamela

It was delightful to hear from you again. I had quite given you up. A lot of girls write letters like yours without seriously intending a meeting. But if you are truly serious, then I can assure you I am too.

For a few minutes after I got your letter my mind was in chaos. "There must be chaos in the mind if we wish to breed a dancing star" —do you know who said that? A great man. I thought, shall I reply? And I cannot tell you all the ideas that coursed through my mind, but what I had was a kind of *vision* of you. A forehead high and noble, eyes of deepest blue, a sweep of fair hair. Was the vision true or false? And are you true or false, Pamela?

I thought also: Is she the kind of girl who is right for initiation, does she know how close suffering is to joy? And that the supreme moment in life is the one when fantasy becomes reality? If you think these things are interesting, then we have a lot to offer you. Our aim is to obtain supremacy over the ordinary things in life. We are *not ordinary human beings*, my woman friend and I. It is a question whether you have the ability to join us where we live on a higher plane of pleasure.

I have told you something of myself. You know I am an older man than you. It would not be convenient for me to come up to London, and anyway our meeting place is in Rawley. You say you might be able to come down. If so, tell me what evening, and I will meet you at 9 o'clock outside a tobacconist's shop called Eastham, in Station Road.

The address on the envelope will find me for the next few days. I hope to meet you, Pamela, I hope you can join us.

Abel

An addressed manila envelope was enclosed. The address was: A. Giluso, Batchsted Farm, East Road, Sutton Willis.

Pamela showed it to Sally in the salad bar they sometimes used for lunch. Sally shivered. "There's something nasty about it. Do you think he's mad?"

"I'll tell you what it sounds like to me—some sort of black magic group. You know, you all dance around naked and then somebody dressed up as the devil screws what's supposed to be a virgin on an altar."

"Have you been to one?"

"As a matter of fact I haven't. It might be fun."

Sally read the letter again. "Giluso. What do you suppose he is, Italian?"

"Could be. Or Maltese."

"He's got your hair right, hasn't he? And I suppose you do have a high forehead. Not your eyes, though; they're green."

"Greeny-bluey." Pamela speared a bit of cottage cheese. "What do you say we go along together. Then we can jump out on him and say, 'Boo, Mr. Giluso, here's two girls come to be initiated.'"

"I don't know, Pam. Perhaps we ought to go to the police. I mean, Louise was killed in Rawley, and she did write to this man."

"So she wrote to him. I don't suppose Mr. Giluso's got anything at all to do with her being killed; he's just a dirty old man getting his kicks. Very likely he won't turn up at all. But if he does, sweetie pie, we protect each other, don't we? And if we find out anything we tell the police and they clap hands. How about Friday, can you manage that?"

"I suppose so."

"And perhaps he's just a lovely sexy Italian with—" Pam whispered and Sally giggled. Pam certainly made everything fun.

Plender had asked for an interview with Lowson at the office simply to get background information on Vane. What he learned, as he said afterward, shook him rigid, and he rang Hazleton at once. The DCI told him to talk to both the girls involved, find out just what had happened and whether they'd received any letters at any time from Abel. The results, as Plender said on the following day, were disappointing.

"Joy Lindley, that's the girl at the office, all he did was take her out for a couple of drinks. Never so much as kissed her, so she said, and I believe her. The other girl, Monica Fowler, there was a bit of feeling around, and he exposed himself to her, and that's all, or so she says. Of course you've got to remember she was thirteen at the time, and it was four years ago. She didn't much want to talk about it. Her parents were cagey too. In effect they blackmailed Vane, and he was fool enough to let them. I think they're feeling sorry they raised the whole thing again."

"No letters to either of them?"

"None. And they didn't call him Abel, never heard the name in relation to him."

"So what do you think?"

"Hard to say, sir. Doesn't sound like a killer to me, more like the sort of poor sod who fumbles about with little girls behind the bushes. I'll tell you what Lowson did say, though. Vane's work has been unsatisfactory lately. I gather they're thinking of sending him on some refresher course or other."

"Paul, sit down. This isn't going to be agreeable." Bob Lowson's voice was unusually muted. "I had the police round here making inquiries about you today. A man named Plender, from Rawley."

"I see."

As Lowson went on speaking with this unaccustomed solemnity, his features became more piglike. "The inquiries were in relation to the death of that girl Louise Allbright."

"Yes. They found a letter which they think was typed on a machine of mine, I can't imagine how."

"I don't want to know the details, Paul. What I have to tell you is this. Plender asked me for any other information—*any* other information—about your conduct and character. I had to tell them about that girl, the one whose parents wrote to Brian. It seemed to me that otherwise I might be accused of concealing information. I'm afraid they'll ask some more questions. I'm sorry."

"I understand." The tic in Vane's face was working again. "I see that you had to tell them."

"Something else. It's been obvious to me, and to other people too, I expect, that for the past few weeks you've been under strain. There've been several little things like—oh, that business about the lavatories—where I've thought your judgment hasn't been quite at its best."

"The cleaning has gone back to the old system. All toilet rolls now present and correct." Paul essayed a laugh.

"That was just an instance. There are other things."

Vane's whole body drooped, as though a new, shrunken inhabitant had come to live in the well-cut clothes. Lowson felt personally sorry for him, but such feelings had nothing to do with business.

"Once the police have started digging, I don't know what they may turn up. What there is for them to turn up. Nothing, I hope." The telephone light on his desk flickered. He snapped at his secretary that he was not to be disturbed. "It's been suggested that you should go on one of those courses mentioned at the Job Enrichment discussion, a Jay Burns Lawrence course it's called. Do you know about them?"

"I know they're the kind of thing where you play leadership games and afterward they tell you your attitude's all wrong. No, thank you."

"Paul, I don't think you quite understand the position. I've been in your corner, I said to Brian that a man's private life is his own affair, but with the police coming in we're past that. You can go on this course. It starts next Monday, lasts for a couple of weeks. Then we'll reconsider when it's over. Or you can go on leave for a month, and after that we'll see."

"You don't give me much choice, do you? Who'll take over my department? Esther, I suppose."

"For the time being, Esther, yes. It isn't a good idea for you to be around the office at the moment, not for you or for the organization."

"Yes, let's not forget the organization."

"Don't make it too difficult for me, Paul."

"If I go on the course, what happens afterward?"

"I'll do everything I can."

Paul Vane got up, and his suit was refilled with his personality as though he were a slack balloon into which gas had been pumped. His smile was the one that Bob Lowson had always found attractive. "Thanks. I suppose the thing to do is to do so marvelously on this bloody silly course that even the Brian Hartfords can scarce forbear to cheer. I know where all these ideas come from, Bob, and it's not from you. Thank you for breaking it gently."

Lowson was relieved. He liked Paul when he behaved properly. He moved back a picture to show a safe let into the wall, twirled the dials and opened it to reveal a cupboard filled with bottles. They drank a large whisky to the Jay Burns Lawrence course.

Five minutes later Joy Lindley passed Paul Vane in the corridor. She was going to stop and say that she was sorry if she'd caused him trouble and that she hadn't meant to do so, but he went by as though she were not there.

Paul accepted Alice's bridge playing without complaint, although he did say that he thought she might be at home when he came back in the evening. When she asked with controlled ferocity, "What for?" he had no ready answer.

"I find bridge absorbing; it occupies my mind. I used to play when I was in college. You didn't know that?"

"No. I remember playing with you later on, but I didn't know you took it seriously."

"You don't know anything about me before I met you. I played bridge a lot, and I was very good." She glared at him. "I provide food for you; what more do you want?"

"Let's not quarrel. You play bridge."

On the night after his conversation with Bob Lowson, then, he was not surprised to find the house empty. A casserole had been left in the oven. He ate some of the stew, and was about to go back to his work on the wine racks when the bell rang.

Plender said, "Good evening, Mr. Vane."

He stood aside to let the sergeant in, but Plender shook his dark head. "Mr. Hazleton would be glad if you could come down to the station."

"To the station."

"Just to clear up one or two points. He thought it would be easier there. My car's outside."

Plender watched the man. He put up a hand to his throat as though his collar were tight, but showed no surprise and made no objection.

Paul Vane had been in a police station only once before in his life, to report the theft of his car radio. He was surprised by the casualness of it all, the men standing about and chatting rather as though it were a clubroom. At the moment he came into the station the desk sergeant was saying to an old woman carrying a shopping basket, "So it's you again, is it, my old duck? And what have we got this time?" She responded by saying something causing a roar of laughter, in which she joined.

"What's she here for?" Paul asked.

"Shoplifting. One of our regulars." They made a right-angled turn down a corridor. It might be our own offices, he briefly thought. Then Plender tapped on a door and they were inside the room. A room perhaps fourteen foot square, containing a desk, green filing cabinets, pictures of police sports on the dingy gray walls. Hazleton got up from behind the desk. His face was shiny, his hand hard and hot.

"Good of you to come down. One or two things we thought could best be cleared up down here." Looking around at this bare hostile room, Vane wondered what things could possibly be cleared up in a place like this. How could the people who worked here understand the motives of fellow humans? "This is Chief Superintendent Paling."

The silver-haired man with refined features and a mean mouth did not shake hands but nodded to him. He sat away and to the back of Hazleton, conveying the impression of being a neutral observer. Both men looked at him in what seemed an expectant way. He found it necessary to speak.

"I suppose it's about the typewriter."

"The typewriter. Yes, let's start with that," Hazleton said heartily. "Perhaps you'd like to make a statement saying just what you know about it. What you said the other night, with anything else you can remember. Talk to the sergeant over there. Take your time."

Plender was by the door, a notepad on his knee. Paul Vane talked with composure. When he had finished Hazleton nodded. "That's what you said before."

"There's nothing else to say."

"Here's a photostat of the letter typed on your machine. Mean anything to you?"

He started to read. "This wasn't to Louise Allbright."

"I never said it was. It was to the French au pair who's disappeared."

"Then perhaps it's got no connection with the other thing."

"I didn't say it had. I asked if it meant anything to you."

"Nothing at all."

"How about the name Abel. Know anyone called Abel? Any suggestions?"

"Only that it's a French name rather than English. And the girl was French too. I remember a French film director named Abel Gance."

122

"So how did Abel, whether he was French or English, get hold of your typewriter?"

"I've told you, I don't have any idea. I can only suggest it was while it was at the house, before we moved in."

"Come along now, Mr. Vane." Hazleton's manner had changed suddenly to one of sneering disbelief. He looked like a bulldog ready to bite. "Are you telling us that somebody looking round your house *just happened* to spot your Olivetti and thought: How convenient, I'll sit down and write a letter on this bit of paper I *just happen* to have in my pocket? Are you telling us that? Because it sounds to me like a load of poppycock."

Vane looked surprised but not frightened. "I'm not telling you anything. I said I couldn't explain it."

The DCI pointed a finger like a ramrod. "Instead of that poppycock, try this. It was your machine. You typed the letter. Then you took the chance of unloading it on your daughter—"

"My stepdaughter."

"Let me finish." He seemed to be in a towering rage. "Then you met this girl, and what happened after that? It wasn't the first of those Abel letters, was it? Supposing I told you we had other letters typed on that same Olivetti of yours; what would you say then?"

Vane's voice was calm. He even managed a smile. "I should say I'd never met the au pair girl in my life, and that if you had other letters you'd have shown me copies. And, Inspector, remember I'm used to dealing with people. I know when somebody's blustering about, trying to browbeat me. It's foolish. And, if you don't mind my saying so, old-fashioned."

Hazleton flung himself back in his chair, so that it creaked slightly. Paling, soft-voiced, took up the questioning.

"When Sergeant Plender came round to see you, Mr. Vane —you remember that?"

"Of course."

"Your wife said you took an interest in young girls. What did she mean?"

"Nothing." His smile flashed on and quickly off again like a lighthouse signal.

"Did she say it because she knew about Monica Fowler?" He watched to see the effect. Vane didn't like it, but he had been told, he was ready for the question.

"She did know about Monica Fowler."

"She was a girl of thirteen."

"Yes."

"Did you have sexual relations with her?"

"No. I felt affectionately to her like . . . an uncle." Hazleton snorted. Paling glanced at him disapprovingly. "They accused me of doing all sorts of things. I hadn't done them, but I was stupid, I paid some money."

"Two hundred pounds for their silence. I see you don't agree, but it was for their silence, wasn't it?"

"If you put it that way."

"How would you put it?" Paling asked pleasantly. "The charge would have been indecent assault. You paid and the matter was dropped."

"They'd never have brought a charge." Vane's face was very pale.

"Then why pay?" He did not answer. "Then her family wrote to your wife."

"Yes."

"But that wasn't the only time, was it? Tell us about the other times."

"There's—there was—was only one other time."

"Tell us about it."

"A girl named Sheila—Sheila Winterton. It was seven years ago. We knew her family. Sheila wanted some tuition in French. I used to be good at languages; I gave it to her."

"And what happened?" Vane muttered. "I didn't hear that."

"Alice was doing a part-time job then. She came back one day and found us."

"How old was Sheila?"

"Twelve." He added in a voice that was almost inaudible, "That was the only other time, I swear, the only time." He put his head on the table. His shoulders shook with weeping.

Paling wrinkled his nose. Such scenes were disagreeable, but one had to soldier on. His voice was very gentle. "What about Louise? Tell us about her."

Vane raised his tear-stained face, the tic working in his cheek. "Nothing about Louise Allbright. I hardly knew her, I kissed her good night once—how many times do I have to say it?"

Paling got up, moved behind Vane. Plender got up too, and moved behind him on the other side. Hazleton wagged his finger again, but this time in a cheerful admonitory way. "Temper, temper."

In the next moment Plender put his dark curly head close to Vane's ear. "That's not what she said to her parents. She said you wanted to make love and she didn't."

Hazleton leaned over. "Kissing isn't your line, is it? You wanted to show her all you'd got, even though it didn't amount to much. That's what put her off, right?"

"You got a woman to help you out," Plender said. "You thought three would be better than two, stir you up a bit. Then it went wrong."

Vane turned round and screamed at his tormentor. "No, no, it wasn't like that."

"Right then, tell us what it was like, how it happened."

"That isn't what I mean. I can't do it, I haven't been able to for years, I couldn't do anything if I wanted."

Paling quietly opened the door and went out. The cat-and-mouse process of interrogation was one he had never cared for, although he knew it to be necessary. When he went back more than an hour later, however, Vane had made no admission. His tie was to one side, his elegant dark suit had lost some of its shape although he had not been touched, the mark of dried tears was on his face. Paling thanked him for his cooperation and sent him home in a police car.

"He doesn't smell like a killer to me," Hazleton said afterward. "There's a stink, but not the right stink. By God, it's hot." He had taken off his jacket, and there were sweat marks at the back of his shirt and under his arms.

"There's the typewriter."

"Yes. So what do we do?"

"We go on keeping an eye on him. All the time. If a girl or woman is involved he must meet her somewhere, sometime. And put on a little pressure, let him know he's being watched."

When Paul Vane got home, Alice was playing through a bridge hand from a book. She was smoking one of her little cigars, and three stubs were in an ashtray. He told her that he was being sent on a special course on the following Monday, and also that he had been down at the police station answering questions.

"I just don't want to know. There's a time when I would have been interested, but not now."

"I tell you I'm liable to lose my job."

"You'll get another."

"The police accused me of killing that girl. And the Services' au pair. More or less, they accused me."

"It's a hot night." She took off her dress, stood in bra and briefs. "Do anything to you?"

"You know I didn't touch her, you must know that."

She shrugged and sat down again. "I believe you can only make this contract if you leave the lead with dummy and finesse the club."

"Alice."

"Why should you say I know? I don't know anything about you, you don't know anything about me. If you're going to the kitchen you might get me a glass of lemon squash. I'm thirsty."

That was Thursday evening.

18

Extracts from a Journal

■■■■■ ■■■ ■■■ ■■■ ■■■ ■■■ ■■■ ■■■ ■■■ ■■■ ■■■ ■■■ ■■■ ■■■ ■■■ ■■■

JULY

I look at the last notes I made and ask again the question: Who are these words written for? Answer: Myself. Yes, but for an audience too. I am addressing *somebody,* and I do not know who it is. My Ideal Reader will understand all, forgive all. Yes, I am in no doubt that there are things to forgive.

But most of all the Ideal Reader will appreciate my cleverness. A Game well played, he will say, and I see him burst into applause. People do not know my cleverness. That galls. The Master said:

> This fame, which all the wide world loves,
> I touch with gloves,
> And scorning beat
> Beneath my feet.

Yet Friedrich Nietzsche too longed for the appreciation of a friend, one friend. Consider those chapter headings in *Ecce Homo*: "Why I Am So Wise," "Why I Am So Clever," "Why I Write Such Excellent Books." Like the Master I write for one person who will understand. That cannot be Bonnie. She is a fool, a tool, nothing more. She serves sensation. I use it, rise above it.

127

Last night Clayton appeared to me in a dream, as he has not done for years. We went swimming together, the water deep deep blue (I knew the water was blue although I could not see it; I have never seen a color in a dream). I was swimming underwater and I could see Clayton's legs waving like pale fronds. Then they disappeared. Something fastened round my neck. I knew it to be Clayton's hands, fought and thrashed to be free. At last I woke, shivering uncontrollably and with my pajamas wet.

I thought of Clayton, my beloved brother. The clever one.

In our room at the top of the house, the attic room with my bed tucked under the sloping ceiling so that I bumped my head if I sat up quickly, Clayton tormented me with riddles.

Question: Would you sooner be a bigger fool than you look, or look a bigger fool than you are?

Answer: Both are impossible.

Clayton knew dozens, hundreds of riddles. I was so silly that I always tried to answer them. But at school, and when other people were there, he protected me and was kind. You must look after your little brother, they said, and Clayton said yes. You must obey your brother, they said, and I said yes. Clayton protected me. When I was seven, boys were tormenting me in the lavs, two holding me, two playing with my thing. Then Clayton appeared, sudden and terrible like a god. Clayton scattered them, kicking and punching.

Clayton like a god. If I was seven he was nine. A nine-year-old god.

Like a god he demanded worship. Kneel down, Clayton said, and I knelt. In the attic room I worshiped him with my hands, my mouth. He was a cruel god. Sometimes I kissed his feet.

How can one kill a god? It is impossible.

From his position above me on the cliff, secure on a ledge, Clayton looked down. I was stuck, and cried. "Crybaby," he said. "Stupid little crybaby, frightened of the rocks."

128

The sea was blue below.

"Crybabies have to be punished. Crybabies must learn to climb." He came down three or four steps on the rocks, easy and graceful, stretched his hand to help me up. I took the hand and pulled.

A piece of rock broke away and dropped down slowly. Clayton's feet scrabbled. He let go of my hand and I saw him pass me. He made no sound. A god does not cry. I saw his body in air.

Why did he not take me with him? Because he was a god. Why did I afterward scramble to safety quite easily?

Did I mean to pull him down? They thought so. They did not speak to me for a week after the funeral. The attic room was mine. There were no more acts of worship. Clayton died when he was twelve years old. There was no blood.

It is the instinct of man to destroy his gods. But they are indestructible, in some form or other they always return.

Do I hate women? No. But I have in my mind not only the Ideal Reader but the Ideal Woman, lovely and obedient. For a woman the man must be her god, as Clayton was mine.

I imagine this little Pamela who has written to me. Her features are small and delicate like her fingers, her hair is fair as that of a Rhine maiden. Most of all she has understanding, her vision sees beyond what is trivial, she is searching for a communion of minds. She desires the flesh, but through it sees the spirit.

Bonnie does not live upon this plane. Her mind is intent always upon the lower things. All she wants is blood, there is nothing else in her mind. I may have to protect Pamela from her as Clayton protected me from those rough boys long ago. Then Pamela will make her act of worship. She will kiss my feet.

Bonnie has no conception of the infinite. She does not understand the Game, at times she treats it as a joke. Bonnie is my lower nature.

129

19

What Happened on Friday

━━ ━━ ━━ ━━ ━━ ━━ ━━ ━━ ━━ ━━ ━━ ━━ ━━ ━━ ━━ ━━ ━

Detective Constable Billy Paterson was twenty-three, a tall cheerful ruddy officer whose interests were rugby football, beer and girls in that order. He was the best front row forward in the police team, and one of the two hardest drinkers. He was not noted for his subtlety, and he was an ideal man for the task of making himself conspicuous.

On Friday morning he was waiting with a colleague at the end of the road when Paul Vane came out of his drive in his car, which he left at the station. Paterson was dropped off there, and traveled up in the same compartment as Vane. During the morning he made his identity known to the doorman at Timbals and sat in the entrance hall reading comics. At lunchtime Vane went out to a pub, ate a sandwich and drank two large whiskies. Paterson was around the other side of the bar nursing a pint of bitter, and Vane noticed him for the first time. On the way back to the office he looked around to see if Paterson was following.

Paterson made a bit of a variation in the routine by spending most of the afternoon in a coffee bar opposite the office. He had obtained a fresh stock of comics, which he found irresistibly amusing, so that he was not bored. It did not take much to amuse him. Indeed, his only worry about this particular job was that he believed Friday to be his unlucky day for tailing suspects. The worry was based on the undoubted fact that he had twice lost suspects he had been tailing on that day.

Vane left the office at a quarter to six, and Paterson trailed after him. Again he sat in the same compartment. As they left Rawley station Vane stopped as though about to speak, and then walked on. A squad car was waiting for Paterson, and they followed Vane home. They saw him go in, then parked down the road.

"You staying?" Paterson asked.

His companion was Tiny Noble, a saturnine figure in his thirties who was disappointed that he had missed promotion.

"No need for two of us to waste our bloody time. I'll be back at ten to relieve you."

Noble was collected five minutes later. Paterson settled down happily with another comic.

The house was unwelcoming. Cigar butts lay in the ashtrays, the washing up had not been done, there was nothing in the oven. Alice was evidently playing bridge. Paul Vane looked out through the front window at the car parked down the road. He felt as uneasy as though some small animal were crawling over his skin. He looked in the larder for something that could be heated for supper, but could not face the thought of doing it.

The note was on the living room table.

Paul

I am going away. Sorry, but it's the only way. If the police are going to ask questions about those girls I can't take it, why should I? That and everything else. I have tried, though you may not think so. I don't think there's any use in trying to pick up the pieces. We're just incompatible, that's all.

Didn't have time to cook anything for you. Suggest you go out and eat at that new place you mentioned the other day.

Alice

P.S. Have told Jennifer. She wasn't surprised.

He read the words with the disbelief people feel for something contemplated so often that they have become sure it will never happen. Alice never played jokes, yet he felt that some sort of joke was being played here and that he would find her working out a bridge problem—perhaps in Jennifer's bedroom? He actually went in there and looked around. Then he went into their own bedroom, looked at the empty dressing table and, as though unconvinced, opened drawers, flung closet doors dramatically wide. Clothes had been taken, but not everything had gone. He found a kind of comfort in the fact that she had made the beds. Would she have done that if she were not secretly intending to return? Perhaps she had put the clothes down in the cellar to add to the shock he was receiving? Perhaps the suitcases were still down there.

He went down to the cellar. The suitcases had gone.

Zook-zlook-*glook*, said Porgity Bear as he saw the swaying rump of Lavinia May moving down the High Street. Holy *daggity*, he thought as she turned into Charlie Beast's, where Bolo Bunny was playing Big Chief Firewater for the mineral rights on Sharkfire Island. Porgity Bear ran up the wall, peered in the window at Charlie Beast's. Dumbfounding doggerel, he cried. What he saw inside made him relax his hold on a drainpipe. He teetered over space.

What had Porgity seen? Billy Paterson turned the page in delight. He was suddenly aware of an alien sound, and in the next moment Vane's Cortina moved past him and made a left turn with a shriek of tires. Cursing, he started the engine, which did not fire until the second attempt, turned the car and followed down Burgess Road. The Cortina was a quarter of a mile ahead of him, and had made another left turn.

Paterson looked at his watch. Twenty forty-three, and the light was beginning to fail. He drove with one hand, lifted the telephone with the other, made radio contact and gave his position. To do this he slowed down fractionally as he made the left turn into Cary Avenue. He was appalled to see that there was no Cortina ahead. Roads led off Cary Avenue to left and right, and he had to cut his speed to look down them. He did not see the Cortina. The end of Cary Avenue ran into London Road one way, Manholt Place the other. Cars were passing. He did not know which way the Cortina had gone.

He spoke to HQ. "Paterson. I've lost contact."

The duty officer was a short-tempered man named Pink. "You've what? You were parked outside his bloody house."

"He shot out like a bomb. By the time I'd turned—"

"You'll have a bomb under you, lad, when the chief gets word of this. Give me his number. Then cruise around, keep in touch, try not to fall asleep at the wheel."

Tailing a man on Friday, Paterson thought, I might have known. He folded the Porgity Bear comic, the cause of his trouble, and was about to throw it out of the window. He tucked it into his raincoat pocket instead, and started to move down London Road.

The tobacconist's was shut, like the other shops in Station Road. There was not much traffic. It was almost dark. Sally said, "He's not coming."

"It's only just nine. Don't be so fidgety, sweetie pie. If Abel Giluso appears there are two of us to deal with him."

"Have you got the letter?"

"Of course." She took it out of her large fabric bag. "I shall produce it, say, 'You are Abel Giluso, my name is Pamela Sexpot and I claim the right to move on to a higher plane of pleasure.' I mean, did you ever hear anything so corny?" Pamela's makeup was smooth as enamel, her hair glinted golden, her miniskirt showed elegant legs.

"I don't know about corny. It frightens me."

"You haven't seen my magic protector. I don't mean the pill." She delved into the bag and came up with a police whistle. "One blast on this and Abel will take to his heels."

"There's something funny about this road."

"Oh, sweetie, be your age. It's a perfectly ordinary road, so ordinary it's boring." Two boys on the other side whistled, then crossed. A passing car slowed momentarily, speeded up again.

The boys were about sixteen. Their small cunning faces looked out from a forest of hair. One of them said, "What's up?" and the other, "If you're looking for it I've got it."

Sally was not used to being accosted by the vulgar. She turned her back on them. Pamela said, "Sorry, boys, I'm waiting for a man."

"What's he got that I haven't?" the first boy said. He put a hand on Pamela's arm. "Come on, and I'll show you."

"Just a minute." She produced the whistle from her bag. "Shall I blow it?"

The boys stared disgustedly. "You must be out of your mind," one of them said. They slouched off down the street.

"It's a quarter past. I'm going home. You come back too, Pam, and have supper."

"You don't suppose one of them was really our Abel, do you?"

"I don't know and I don't care. I hate this. Come back with me; there's a spare bed."

"Just give it five minutes. Don't you want to see what he looks like? What's the betting he's a hunchback, or can't get out a sentence without stuttering? Would you fancy being done by a hunchback? I mean, it might be different."

Most of the time Sally admired almost everything about Pamela—her sexual freedom, her outspokenness, the whole way she lived—but just occasionally she felt disgusted, as she did now. She began to walk away.

At the corner she turned. Pamela was standing beside the shop, lighting a cigarette. She waved and blew a kiss.

Five minutes later the car that had slowed when the boys were talking to them came round the corner, slowed again and stopped. Pamela went to the window. "Mr. Giluso?"

"You'll be Pamela." He leaned over, opened the front door. She got in. He drove away.

"You're not at all as I thought you'd be," she said.

He looked at her briefly. "Neither are you. At least, I don't think so."

"I mean, no hunchback."

"Hunchback?"

"Just a joke." She became aware that somebody was in the back of the car, turned. "It's a little party, is it? Where are we going?"

"Why did you bring somebody else with you?"

She turned back toward the driver, and so never saw the pad that was pressed firmly over her mouth and nostrils from behind.

20

Extracts from a Journal

▬ ▬ ▬ ▬ ▬ ▬ ▬ ▬ ▬ ▬ ▬ ▬ ▬ ▬ ▬ ▬ ▬ ▬ ▬ ▬

SATURDAY, JULY 23

Why is what seems like fulfillment disappointing, so that in the end it is not fulfillment at all? I have looked for the answer to this from the Master, but have not found it. Yet surely he knew such sorrows, the joys that turn to ash, better than any man who has ever lived.

The girl Pamela. I read what I wrote about her only a day or two ago. "She has understanding, her vision sees beyond what is trivial," etc. All wrong, wrong. She was nothing but triviality, mere modern rubbish.

I am copying here part of the tape that we made. Bonnie is keeping the tape. It gives her the most passionate pleasure. I cannot say that it gives such pleasure to me, but I note it down. In a sense Pamela's triviality is our justification.

We had set everything up. She was tied in a suitable manner. I have noted only part of the tape, there was a great deal more.

Dracula: What you have to understand, Pamela, is that you are in a communion with us that is something quite new. You are entering a different world from any you have ever known.

Pamela: Oh, stop talking such balls. If you want kinky sex, let's get on with it.

136

Bonnie: You see. Let me—

Dracula: No, Bonnie.

Pamela: What is it? What's she want to do with me?

Dracula: Pamela. I want you to understand.

Pamela: I'm not a lizzie, but I don't mind trying—

Dracula: Listen to me. The communion Bonnie and I want is not sexual, though sex may enter it. It is religious. Try to understand. Can you imagine being subjected to torments, and rising through and beyond them to another plane of being, to utter peace? Can you imagine the total joy when fantasy becomes reality? You remember, I asked you that in my letter.

Pamela: Yes.

Dracula: Tell me, what is your greatest, deepest fantasy?

Pamela: Oh, I don't know. Being able to go to Yves Saint-Laurent's autumn show and order all the clothes I want. Going in the Royal Box at Ascot, and everyone noticing me. Going to bed with a man on a yacht, and it turns out he's a millionaire, and makes me a present of the yacht.

Dracula: Is that all?

Pamela: I could think better if I was free.

Dracula: Nothing else, nothing higher?

Pamela: I don't know. I don't know what you want me to say.

Dracula: We don't want you to say anything, it is what you want to say. Let me tell you something. I am Count Dracula. She is Bonnie Parker.

Pamela: You're mad. *(A scream)* What's she doing, keep her away. Oh.

Bonnie: Bonnie likes the sight of blood, you see. It excites her. I'll kiss it, that nasty cut.

Pamela: Keep away from me. Please keep her away from me.

Dracula: Keep away.

Bonnie: It's what we're here for, isn't it?

Dracula: No, no. Pamela, don't you understand anything of what I've been saying? Do you know what is meant by the

137

pain barrier? Athletes feel it, and if they are great they go beyond it and find themselves somewhere where pain doesn't exist. Is it a fantasy to think that you can get beyond pain? For those athletes it is true, they make that fantasy become reality. That is what we are trying to do. When does pain become pleasure, and pleasure become pain? Consider all this as a game, and yourself as one of the players.

Pamela: Oh Christ, Christ, get me out of this.

(A scrabbling sound then, her attempt to run out of the room with her legs hobbled, a thud as she is pushed to the floor)

Dracula: You see, don't you? I am your superior. I order, you obey.

Pamela: Only because you've tied my legs, you bastard.

Dracula: The circumstances do not matter, it is the fact that matters. Have the vision to see yourself as a slave.

Bonnie: Come *on*. Let's do something.

Dracula: You do not understand. Crawl across the floor to me, Pamela. Kiss my feet.

Those last words I spoke gently, a good master to his servant. They were rewarded by a flood of filthy abuse which I shall not transcribe. Indeed, I shall put down nothing more. What happened excited and disgusted me, but it was a disappointment. The Game should be a Thing-in-itself, the image of a perfect Reality. Yet it always fails.

Comments and Reflections. I said before that there was sex in what we did, and it must be exorcised. Did we do that here? I cannot remember.

The tape recorder. A failure. Bonnie does not think so, she is keeping it to gloat over and replay. But I shall not permit its use again. I am shocked by what the tape says. It does not tell the truth I hoped for.

Bonnie. She has a kind of blood lust. My aim is purity, the

perfect relationship, hers is to cut and maim. Was this once my aim too? Yes, but something more. Bonnie takes only her own satisfaction seriously, not the Theory of the Game. That is not permissible. It must be stopped.

Last night she laughed at me, asked why Dracula did not play his proper vampire's part. But it is the Theory that stirs me, its abstract perfection. I do not like the taste of blood.

All this written on the following day, Saturday, in deepest depression. Uncertain of intentions, desires, whether to go on. By ordinary standards what I have done is "wrong." Do those standards matter? The Master says: "All 'evil' actions are motivated by the instinct of self-preservation, or still more accurately, by the individual's eye to pleasure and to the avoidance of pain; but as motivated in this way they are not evil." Or again he speaks of the lonely man who conceals his thoughts and lives in the cave of his imagination. "From time to time, we take revenge for our violent concealment, for our enforced restraint. We come out of our cave with frightening looks, our words and deeds are then explosions, and it is possible that we collapse within ourselves. In such a dangerous fashion do I live."

I am that violent concealed man, I am Friedrich Nietzsche. And you out there, all you others, are not you also concealed in your caves?

21

The End of Friday

■■ ■■ ■■ ■■ ■■ ■■ ■■ ■■ ■■ ■■ ■■ ■■ ■■ ■■ ◀

It was after eleven o'clock when the bell rang. Norah Parkinson looked at her husband. "That man."

The Brigadier had been occupied with the *Times* crossword. At her words he made a feebly negative gesture, as though it would silence the bell.

"No doubt he wants to create a brawl. You must send him away."

"I don't quite see—"

"Charles. Must I go myself?"

The bell rang again. "I don't know what to say."

"Just get rid of him."

The door revealed Paul Vane. "Well," the Brigadier said with apparent surprise. "It's you, Paul." His son-in-law stared at him. "What sort of a night is it?" He went outside, sniffed the air, looked up at the stars. "Fine night. How are you, Paul, my boy."

"Is Alice here?"

It struck the Brigadier for the first time that Paul was not entirely sober. The outer signs were not great, some disarrangement of the hair, distinctly dirty shoes, a wild look, but the fact was unquestionable to somebody who had seen as many men three sheets in the wind as had the Brigadier. "Alice," he said like a man naming a strange animal. "You're looking for Alice."

"Are you going to ask me in?"

"Of course, Paul. It's just—"

They were in the hall. The drawing room door opened, framing Norah. She advanced, glaring. "What do you want?"

"Just to know if Alice is here. I want to talk to her."

She glared in the direction of the stairs, as though calculating the possibility of interposing her body if Paul made a dash for them. Then she said unwillingly, "We can't talk out here."

The Brigadier trotted behind them, happy that decision had been taken out of his hands. "Spot of whisky?" he suggested. The words were ignored.

"Alice is here, then."

"She is in bed. She has taken a sedative. I should not think of disturbing her." Advancing on Paul, and positively swelling a little as she did so, she said, "Alice has left you for good. From what she's told me, I'm not surprised."

"What do you mean?"

"The schoolchildren." She averted her eyes. "And now you have mixed yourself up in this unsavory affair. I think she has been very forbearing."

Paul Vane raised his arm. Norah stepped back, giving a refined scream. The Brigadier moved forward and clutched the arm. "Now then, Paul, old man—"

"Let go of my arm—what the hell's the matter with you?" He jerked his arm free. "She's my wife. I want to talk to her."

"Alice is asleep. I absolutely forbid it." Norah moved to stand in front of the door. "If you want to communicate with her you can write a letter. Or telephone. But I doubt if she will speak."

Paul Vane looked so miserable, so utterly lost and hopeless, that the Brigadier was moved to pity. "Couldn't we, my dear—after all, Paul has his rights—"

"No." As though sensing that the danger was over, she moved from the door. "Alice is overwrought. I will not have her disturbed." She accompanied him like a bodyguard on his way out of the house.

The Brigadier came too, and put his head through the car window. "Careful how you go. Don't want any accidents. Norah's right, you know, no good talking tonight. Leave things a day or two, you'll find it may all blow over. I mean, women."

The car started, went down the drive. Its taillight disappeared. "You should have let him see her."

His wife scuffed the ground with her shoe. "He's made marks on the gravel."

22

A Hard Saturday

Saturday morning, 0 nine thirty hours. Hazleton's first thought when Vane opened the door was that here was a man going to pieces. It was not just that he was wearing an old shirt and trousers so that his usual appearance of bandbox smartness had gone, or that he was unshaved and smelled of drink. Something more than this showed in the pinched nose and red eyes. Hazleton had seen enough men toppling toward collapse to recognize one now. Just one little push and—what would happen then?

Honesty as the DCI practiced it was always a matter of policy, and he thought it politic to be halfway honest now. He refused to join Vane in the whisky he was drinking, and said, "I won't beat about the bush. Yesterday we had a man watching you. Last night you gave him the slip. Where did you go?"

Vane looked out of the window. "You've called off the hounds."

"For the moment. If we put them on again we'll try to make sure you don't get away so easily. Well, Mr. Vane?"

"Well what?"

"Where were you?"

Vane sloshed the whisky about in his glass. "What the hell business is it of yours? I don't mind saying, but what the hell business is it of the bloody police?" Hazleton waited. Vane pushed a piece of paper toward him. "I found this waiting for me when I got home last night. A nice little welcome."

Hazleton read the letter. "What does it mean, 'That and everything else'?"

"I told you the other night. About . . . not doing it."

"So you did. That's what 'everything else' means, is it? It doesn't mean your wife is worried about your connection with murder."

"Of course it bloody doesn't. You're persecuting me, trying to plant something on me. Somebody's—"

"Yes?"

"Nothing." For a moment the man had looked frightened. Why?

"So you found this note. What did you do?"

"Went out and got drunk."

"Not immediately. You got home before seven, left at a quarter to nine."

"I don't know what the hell I did. Drank. Sat and thought. Then went out so that I could drink with other people."

"You went out at eight forty-three. Our man says you deliberately set out to lose him. Why?"

"It wasn't too difficult." The ghost of a smile flickered around Vane's mouth. "I didn't want to be followed about."

"Nobody else spotted you." Vane shrugged. "You came back at eleven fifty-seven, three minutes before midnight."

"If you say so."

"Where had you been?"

"Drinking. Not in town; that may be why your chaps missed me. I went to a pub out at Pranting, I think it may be called the Spread Eagle, then to another one there, and a couple of others, one near Green Common."

"The Duke's Children?"

"If you say so. I was trying to get drunk. Have you ever tried to get drunk, Inspector, and just not been able to? Are you that human?"

"The pubs close at eleven. It's not an hour's drive back from Green Common."

In Vane's bleary eyes there was a sort of calculation. "I went to call on my military father-in-law and my bitch of a mother-in-law. I wanted to see my wife. And they wouldn't let me. They wouldn't wake her up."

If it had been me I'd have bashed the bedroom door down and dragged her out by her hair, Hazleton thought. "And what time was this?"

"I don't know. Must have been after eleven."

"When you left there you drove straight home."

"I expect so. I told you, I'm hazy."

Hazleton closed his book. "You're staying here for the present, are you? I mean, people in your circumstances sometimes move out to a hotel."

"And you'd like to know which it's going to be." He went over to a desk, picked up a card and dropped it into the detective's hand. "My address from Monday, for the next two weeks." Hazleton read:

> The Jay Burns Lawrence School of Management
> Grattingham Manor
> Hampshire

"Mr. Jay Burns Lawrence runs some imbecilic course for managerial people, full of all sorts of stupid tests. Thanks to your interference in my affairs I'm being sent on it. Following me about. Calling at the office, making insinuations, talking to Lowson, asking him things. You're persecuting me."

Hazleton pocketed the card. "I'll keep this if I may. If I were you I should stop drinking. In preparation for those tests."

Eleven hundred hours. The telephone rang and rang. In the end Sally Lowson put down the receiver. She had made up her mind. She dialed the police station and asked for Chief Inspector Hazleton.

Fifteen hundred hours. Paling was off duty. Hazleton spoke to him on the telephone. "It looks like a real break. A girl who's been in touch with Abel. And we've got an address."

Paling had been trying to make a precise identification of some Roman coins he had bought at a sale. He put them aside with a sigh. Half an hour later he was in the office.

"I talked to this girl Sally Lowson earlier, simply because she was a friend of Gordon," Hazleton began.

"The journalist. Does he come into it?"

"Doesn't look like it. The girl works up in Timbals' London office, father's the managing director. She's got a friend there named Pamela Wilberforce. This Wilberforce girl got hold of one of these sex magazines that introduce singles and couples to each other. Not the ordinary friendship magazines but, you know, the kind of thing they sell in Soho."

"I can't say I do know the kind of thing."

"She had one. Here it is."

The magazine was called *Meet Up*. It consisted solely of numbered advertisements, except for an introductory page about how nice it was for friends to meet, signed "Bert" in facsimile. Paling read:

> E63. ATTRACTIVE SEXY HOUSEWIFE, 25, would like to entertain generous mature men at her comfortable flat. Satisfaction guaranteed. London.
>
> E64. BUSINESSMAN, 30 wants to meet kinky females. Has passion for rubber, TV. Essex.
>
> E65. MY NAME IS STELLA. I am a real doll, and so is my husband. Would you like to watch us, or take part in three-handed fun, either sex. Have own place. London/Sussex.

"What does 'passion for TV' mean? Not a quiet evening at home, I presume."

"I asked Sally Lowson that. Seems it's transvestism. All a kind of code. She thought everyone would know what it meant."

146

"Are they all prostitutes?"

Hazleton shook his head, pointed to the next advertisement.

> E66. HUSBAND AND WIFE, young, sporty, would like to
> meet other couples for sex fun. No kinks, no profession-
> als. North Wales.

"Wilberforce showed the Lowson girl the magazine and they agreed to answer some of the ads. Lowson says it was a joke, but they were half serious if you ask me. Anyway, they answered this one." He turned the pages, pointed to it.

> E203. INTERESTED IN DRACULA? Horror films? Bon-
> nie and Clyde? Gentleman, with lady helper, interested
> in reaching psychological reality by unlocking psychic
> emotional forces would like to hear from ladies. Blank-
> shire, Rawley or district.

"You see the number."

"The one on the envelope in Louise's bag."

"Yes. What happened is that Wilberforce answered the ads. They decided not to go on with it. The reply from E203 was signed 'Abel,' and they thought this particular one was such a good joke they showed it to Louise Allbright because she was always going on about wanting adventure. The Lowson girl knows Allbright wrote to Abel. She doesn't know what happened after that."

"Why didn't she tell us this before? Put it another way, why is she telling us now?" Hazleton had rarely seen the Toff so stirred up. "To know something like this and not to tell us . . ."

"I gather Wilberforce talked her out of it. Why she's come to us now—that's the payoff. They fiddled about on their own. Wilberforce wrote to Abel, got a letter from him, arranged to meet last night outside a shop in Station Road. The idea was that for safety's sake they'd both go along. He didn't turn up, they had a bit of an argument, and Lowson left the other girl standing there. She tried to ring her later Friday night and then this morning, got no reply. Then she got the wind up and rang us. I had a word with Emerson in the Met and they made a call at the Wilberforce girl's flat. The caretaker opened it up. She's not there, and it looks as though she's not been back."

"That letter from Abel. Lowson hasn't got it?"

"No, the other girl kept it. All she remembers is, it was type-written, and that some of the things he said made them laugh. They thought it might be a black magic group, and it does sound like it. Abel enclosed an envelope with an address on it, but she can't remember that either. Or his surname, except that it was Gil or Gal something, and they thought it was Italian or Maltese."

"You don't think she's holding anything back?"

"She's a frightened girl," Hazleton said with satisfaction. "She's told me all she knows."

The Toff was turning the pages of the magazine. "Extraordinary the things people want to do, isn't it? Transvestism, watching other people, doing things in groups. I can't say things like that ever appealed to me. I see that Bert gives an address here for letters, and says that visitors are welcome. Presumably it's where he lives. I think you should get on your horse. From the look of it, we're in for a long weekend."

I like that *we*, Hazleton thought.

Seventeen hundred hours. In fact Hazleton didn't mind working on the weekend. It got him away from weeding the flower beds and clipping the hedge, which he detested. Sergeant Brill, who went with him, had made arrangements to take a girl out that evening, and was not pleased by the idea that he might be working late. Hazleton would have called on Plender, but he was off duty, a fact which proved unfortunate. Had Plender accompanied the DCI arrests might have been made that day, and one life might have been saved.

Brill, Charlie Brill, had a bashed-in rugged face and unfashionably short fair hair. He was an ambitious officer, who was keen to demonstrate his merits to his superiors. In the car he looked at the copy of *Meet Up* carefully.

"You see what the technique for sending on letters is, sir? Quite ingenious. You write to one of these box numbers, stick your letter in a plain envelope, write the box number on the back, post it to Bert in another envelope with his fee. You can write four letters for a pound. Bert opens the envelope addressed to him, extracts his fee, looks at the number on the back of the blank envelope, writes the address, posts the letter. Secrecy preserved from everybody except Bert at 123B Westfield Grove."

Hazleton grunted. "It's the sort of thing that ought to be stopped."

They entered London's southeastern suburbs, went through Bromley, Beckenham and Penge, and came to East Dulwich. They passed through wide tree-shaded roads, where large decaying Victorian houses divided into flats awaited the destructive embrace of the property developer who would convert them into what would be called select residential estates. Westfield Grove was one of these roads. Children playing ball stopped and watched them as they got out of the car. The house was gray brick, with steps leading up to a shabby front door, but 123B proved to be the basement. They went down into an area and knocked.

The door was opened by a pimply boy in his teens, with a sparse growth around the chin. He looked at them without surprise and said, "Yair?"

"I want to speak to Bert."

"Yair." He led the way down a passage into a dusty office that contained a small desk piled high with letters, three kitchen chairs and a filing cabinet. A door opposite the one they had come in by presumably led to the back. The boy sat down at the desk, licked stamps and put them on letters as though his life depended on it.

Hazleton sat on one of the kitchen chairs. Brill asked, "You're not Bert?"

"Nah." He pressed a bell push on the desk three times. "Know what that's for?"

"To call Bert."

"One buzz is a call, two's complaints, three's fuzz."

"Was it that obvious?"

"I seen enough fuzz. I got X-ray eyes for 'em."

The two big policemen made the room seem crowded. Hazleton smiled, in a way that meant nothing good. He got up, walked over to the desk, picked up a bunch of the letters and threw them on the floor. Then he got hold of the boy's ear and pulled hard. The boy howled, tried to rise and made a feeble attempt to punch Hazleton. The DCI twisted one of the boy's arms behind his back.

"Assaulting a police officer, you saw that, Sergeant. Now get out there and stop Bert if he's trying to make a getaway."

Brill had already moved to the door, and his hand was on it when it opened. A small woman, with bright bleached hair, came into the room. She wore spectacles encrusted with what were possibly precious stones, a short tight red dress cut to show considerable cleavage, and matching high-heeled red shoes.

"Where the hell d'you think you're going? And what are you doing to Georgie?" She stood in front of the door.

"Georgie, is it? I don't like his manners." Hazleton sent the boy spinning across the room. He crashed into the filing cabinet. "And just get out of the way, will you. We're looking for Bert."

"I'm Bert. You can shut your mouth; no need to look that surprised. Thing is, most clients don't like the idea of dealing with a woman. It's okay if they come here and see me, but not many do that. The name's Alberta, Bert for short. You're not clients, are you?"

"You know that already." The DCI showed his card. She moved away from the door. "Brill, go through and see what you can find."

"You've got a bleeding nerve." She sat down behind the desk, folded her arms and stayed silent until Brill returned. He shook his head.

"Kitchenette and bedroom, that's all. Single room. No sign of any permanent male occupant."

"I tell you why. There isn't one, not now."

"You mean there was?"

"I turfed him out a couple of weeks ago. His name was Alastair, and he was a layabout. And a pinchfist too; he had the idea that I'd do the work and he'd take the cash and give me an allowance."

"Alastair what?" Hazleton was momentarily diverted.

"I never knew. What do you want?"

"A little information about your business."

"Not local, are you? I've had the locals round. I said to him and I say to you, I run a postal service, that's all, and I'm not responsible for anything outside it. Every page of the mag says it's an offense to send pornography through the post. I can't help it if the silly buggers do it, can I?"

"Look, Miss—what's your name?"

"Norman."

"At present I'm not interested in the way you run your business. How long's it been going, by the way?"

"Just a few weeks. Why?"

"Start it up with this Alastair, did you?"

"No. He was what you might call a transient. Bed and board. Couple of friends gave me the idea. There's a dozen mags like *Meet Up*."

"And from the look of that lot of envelopes you're not doing too badly."

"We meet a need."

"I daresay. So you run it on your own? Just with Georgie here?"

"That's right. Georgie sticks on stamps, posts letters. He's got a couple of friends who come in to help. Otherwise it's just me." She looked at her pink nails. "Do you want Georgie?"

"How could anybody want him? I'll bet his mother doesn't." Georgie moved toward the door. "Just a minute, son. I don't want you, but I do want your name and address. Give it to the sergeant."

When the boy had gone Alberta Norman crossed fat legs. "What can I do for you? I like to keep in with the law." Her voice had a tinny quality that seemed synthetic. Indeed, to Hazleton her whole personality appeared false, as though she were a bad actress. But this was not his immediate concern. "I want the name and address of one of your advertisers."

"They're confidential, or supposed to be," she said, and Hazleton knew there would be no trouble. More than that, he felt that she knew what he had been about to ask.

"I suppose I shall have to give you what you want. Men usually do get what they want, don't they? What's the number?"

"E203."

She opened a box on her desk and started to flick through the cards, took one out and handed it to Hazleton. It was typed, and in the top left-hand corner said E203. On the body of the card was the address: Abel Giluso, Batchsted Farm, East Road, Sutton Willis.

"I'll keep this." She did not protest. "Have you ever met this man Giluso?"

"No, he's never been in. Just sent his money and some letters, like most of 'em. Then I post on the letters, that's all."

"Nice little racket," Brill said appreciatively. "What's in here then?" He had his hand on the filing cabinet. She came around the desk screaming something, and slapped at his arm. Brill was conscious of a thick hot body against his own, then her semiprecious glasses fell off and he stooped to pick them up.

"Come on now, what's in here?"

"That's my business. Anyway, it's locked."

"Come on, come on," the DCI said impatiently. "I'm not worried about any other little games you're up to. Open it up."

She took a key ring from her handbag, unlocked the cabinet. Inside was a collection of sex devices, from oddly shaped and pimpled condoms to massagers, corsets and rubber suits. Brill burst out laughing. "What do you lock these up for? You can buy them in any of the sex supermarkets."

"Georgie and his friends, they play around with them."

It seemed to Hazleton that this was a deliberate diversion.

152

"Giluso. Have you spoken to him on the telephone, had any letters written to you?"

"No. I tell you, all they have to do is fill in the form; there's no need to write."

"Do you keep a record of what letters you send on?" She shook her head. Hazleton pushed his face into hers. "You're in trouble, Bert. A lot of trouble. We want to talk to Giluso, and I think you know where he is, don't you?" She shook her brassy head again. "If you're lying to me, Bert, I'll see you get done. You've got form already, don't tell me you haven't, but I'll really see you get done. Now, how many letters did this Giluso have? And what else do you know about him?"

"I don't know anything. Never seen him, never spoken to him. How many letters? I don't know, maybe half a dozen."

Some smell came from her to the DCI's sensitive nostrils. He felt sure that she was lying.

"You open the letters, don't you?" Brill said. "You're not supposed to, but you do. Then you stick 'em back again. Could be useful for blackmail. I bet you make a nice little bit in black on the side." She shook her head again, took off her glasses and twirled them. "And while we're about it, what's the point of wearing these?" He took them from her, gave them to Hazleton. "Plain glass. I noticed when I picked them up."

Her eyes flickered. "They go with the job. They're the kind of thing people expect me to wear, those who come in. And look here." She opened half a dozen of the letters addressed to her. Sealed envelopes dropped out, with their code numbers on the back for addressing. Pound notes and postal money orders dropped out too. "With money like this coming in, why would I need to try anything else?"

Hazleton felt that he was wasting time. No doubt Bert was playing around in some way or another with pornographic material, but there seemed no point in going through all her files. He picked up the card index on the desk, handed it to Brill.

"That's my living you're taking away."

"Think yourself lucky I'm not taking you as well. If there's nothing we want here you'll get it back."

"It won't do you any good. They're mostly accommodation addresses."

"We'll see."

When the two men had gone Bert Norman reached for the telephone.

Eighteen thirty hours. Sutton Willis was in the southern part of the county, fifteen miles from Rawley. They drove along roads crowded with grim-faced holiday weekenders traveling bumper to bumper as they moved down like lemmings to the sea, then turned off into country lanes. It was still hot, and as Brill looked through the cards he found his fingers sticking to them. When he had finished he put them back in the box.

"Nothing that strikes me, sir, except that a lot of 'em look like accommodation names as well as addresses—the men anyway. John Jones, c/o 84 Abernethy Street, Worcester, that sort of thing. Several Smiths, mostly William. Doesn't look as if the women bother with it; their names sound more likely. Natural enough, I suppose; the men have mostly got wives and families, the women are either on the game or what you might call professional amateurs. My girl's got two or three friends who'd do anything for a fiver."

"Has she now? You want to watch it."

"Liz wouldn't step out of line. She knows if she did she'd be in trouble. Right here for Sutton Willis, I think."

They turned right. Hazleton said thoughtfully, "Abel Giluso. That's not like John Jones. Maybe it's his real name, and he is a foreigner."

Sutton Willis was a dozen houses and a village shop. They asked an old man the way to Batchsted Farm.

"Batchsted Farm you want, is it?"

"You got cloth ears, dad? That's what I asked for," Brill said.

The old man had been about to make some further remark, but he cut it off. "Turn left at the crossroads, half a mile to the right there's a cart track. Farm's along there, you can see it from the road." He turned his back on them.

They turned left at the crossroads down a narrow lane, and slowed down. It was more like a mile than half a mile when they stopped and got out. Hazleton swore.

Beside the cart track a notice board said: *Batchsted Farm. Residence and 3 acres. For Sale by private treaty. Apply J. Darling and Co., Bishopsgate, Rawley.* The notice was old and the paint faded.

Across the fields could be seen what looked like a deserted farm. As they went down the track this impression was proved correct. A solid, ugly brick farmhouse confronted them, its windows blind with boards. Several outbuildings, wooden structures in various stages of decay, surrounded a farmyard where grass grew. A cat delicately picked its way among cans and broken bottles. They walked round the back in silence. There was a pond that looked deep and dirty. Broken fences led to weedy fields. Brill pushed at one of the back doors and it gave.

"We're in," he called, and bent down to look. "Somebody's forced an entry. Not too recent though, by the look of it."

Hazleton was not an impressionable man, but he remembered what they had discovered at Planter's Place, and found himself a little reluctant to enter the farmhouse. Brill had brought a flashlight from the car, and Hazleton let him go ahead, shining it about and making occasional facetious comments.

"Kitchen, I suppose. Smells high enough, doesn't it—who's been eating Gorgonzola? Careful when you tread there, sir; that looks to me like dried turd, and I don't mean dog turd at that. Living room. Someone's made a fire, but it looks like a good while back. Hall and stairs. Hallo hallo, nobody's going to get up *those* stairs in a hurry."

The stairs were broken, with three complete treads missing. When Brill pulled at them another piece came away.

"I don't know what you think, sir, but I should say nobody's been doing anything criminal here lately." The DCI did not comment on this evident truth. Brill's ebullience was getting on his nerves. When they were outside he led the way to the outbuildings, and resolutely pulled open the door of the first. There was a rustling sound. A pair of eyes looked out of the darkness. Then Brill shone his flashlight and a large gray rat blundered past them and disappeared around a corner.

"Now what was he gnawing, some nice bit of tender meat?" said the irrepressible Brill. The torch revealed the carcass of a pigeon. "No, just a bit of nature red in tooth and claw. This was once a coal hole, by the look of it. Shall we try the next?"

But the other outbuildings held nothing more interesting than broken bicycles, bits of tractors, rusty farm tools. When they had finished they stood staring at the derelict place.

"The question is," Hazleton said, "what was the idea of Giluso getting his letters sent here, how did he get them delivered, when did he collect? And where from?" He slapped his thigh. "That For Sale sign. There's some sort of box just by it."

The box was a plain wooden one with a slot in it, of a kind more common in America than in England. There was a lock, which Brill broke with a car spanner. Inside was a letter addressed to Mr. A. Giluso, with the number "E203" on the back. The letter was posted from East Dulwich, obviously by Georgie or Bert. It was signed Estelle, gave a telephone number, and said that she was a real dolly swinger, 21, able to give any man a good time. She didn't live in Sussex but had her own cozy pad in Bayswater. She liked anything kinky, and was sure she would give satisfaction. She would expect a little present.

"That's one dolly swinger who won't fall into Dracula's clutches," Brill said.

Hazleton's patience had worn through. "Brill, this case isn't a joke. It's about a mass murderer. What's the matter?"

Brill could hardly speak. When he could get out the words he said, "Dracula, sir."

"What the hell do you mean?"

"Have you got a bit of paper? There's a pad in the car." He

leaned up against the car door writing, then turned with a wide smile and showed the paper to Hazleton. It said:

Abel Giluso—Bela Lugosi

"It was saying 'Dracula' that put it into my mind. Anagram, you see. There's some use in doing crosswords after all. You remember Lugosi played Dracula quite often. He had those funny eyes; he was in lots of horror films."

Hazleton did not remember. It was years since he had been to a cinema. Brill went on.

"Dracula was a vampire, used to suck his victims' blood. Wasn't there a lot of blood about with the Allbright girl?"

He remembered the cuts and bites. "There was." He stared at the two names and said sourly, "Very clever. It takes us one step back, though, instead of forward. If Abel Giluso's just an assumed name—"

"And it is," Brill said perkily.

The DCI glared at him. "Then it's pretty certain he didn't ever live at this farm. So how did he get his letters directed here?"

Nineteen forty-five hours, Saturday evening. It was still hot. Hazleton was back in his office. He bit ferociously into a roast beef sandwich while listening to a chastened DC Paterson, who had been trying to check on Vane's Friday-night movements.

"Most of what he says is all right, sir, but there seems to be one gap. Left home at twenty forty-three—"

"Lost you two minutes later," the DCI said through bread, beef and mustard.

Paterson sat quietly sweating, hating Hazleton. "Went to the Spread Eagle at Pranting as he said, then the Red Lion outside the village. Landlord recognized his picture. Left about nine-thirty. Then the other pub he mentioned, the Duke's Children at Green Common; that's only seven miles away, but he didn't get there till about ten-thirty. Barman recognized the picture, remembered the time roughly. He's pretty sure it wasn't before ten-fifteen. He left just before eleven, in time to call on his father-in-law. But it doesn't take an hour to drive seven miles."

"He mentioned another pub he might have gone to."

"Not between Pranting and Green Common. I've been in them all. They're mostly for locals, and they recognize strangers."

"Bloody awful beef." Hazleton removed a piece of gristle, and considered. There was perhaps three-quarters of an hour of Vane's time on Friday night left unaccounted for. It did not seem that, with or without a partner, he was likely to have caught and killed Pamela Wilberforce in that time. It was possible, of course, that she was being kept as a prisoner somewhere, but the odds seemed to be that Vane had been telling the truth, and that he made a call at a pub which Paterson had somehow missed, or where he had not been recognized.

He dismissed Paterson and looked at the home address of the estate agent handling Batchsted Farm. *J. N. Darling, Oakdene Cottage, Crampton.* Crampton was about three miles out of town. He bit into another beef sandwich and remembered that he had not told his wife he would not be back for dinner. He became aware also that he had not had the coffee he had ordered. He buzzed the desk.

"Where's that muck you call coffee?"

"On the way, sir."

Thirty seconds later it came in, hot and faintly brown, indistinguishable from tea. A policeman's lot is not a happy one, Hazleton thought, as he telephoned his wife and listened to her expostulations about having cooked his dinner already. Really, though, he loved it.

Twenty hundred hours. Brill was closeted with the postmaster who dealt with the Sutton Willis post, a fussy little bald man who resented having been dragged away from a supper party and game of cards at home.

"The last name we have for Batchsted Farm appears to be Mr. L. J. Elliott. That was four years ago. I presume there has been no later occupier."

"Do you know the farm?"

"Ah—yes."

"Then you know there's been no later occupier, right?"

"That is so, yes."

"What happened to Elliott?"

"He ran—ah—a mushroom farm. Unsuccessful, I'm afraid. He emigrated, if recollection serves, to New Zealand."

"And what would happen to a letter addressed there? Suppose I wrote one; would it get delivered? The place is derelict, but there's a letter box outside."

"I suppose, Sergeant—ah—Brill, this is sufficiently urgent to justify dragging me away from home on Saturday night—"

"It's a matter of life and death," Brill said grandiloquently.

"Oh." The postmaster rubbed his bald head. "The truth is, I'm not quite sure."

Brill said brutally, "We have reason to believe that letters for a Mr. Abel Giluso had been delivered to this derelict farm recently. Anyone with half an eye can see nobody's living there, the place is falling down. We want to know who delivered the letters, and why."

"I see. You want to know the entire procedure that would be followed."

"I'm glad it's got through."

"The letters would arrive at Holting post office. They are then sorted by district. Letters for Sutton Willis would go to Upper Binsted sub-post office. They would be collected by the local postman, Mr. Rogers, for delivery."

"So it's Mr. Rogers I want to see. What's he like?"

"Ted Rogers? He's been in the service for twenty-two years. Rides around everywhere on his bike. I can't remember the last time he had a day off for illness."

" 'Rides around everywhere on his bike,' " Brill mimicked savagely as he drove away. Anybody who did that sort of thing for twenty-two years was in his view a clot who wanted his brains tested. Brill had his own career mapped out. He had been a young sergeant, and he was going to be the youngest

159

inspector on the county force. He would become detective chief superintendent. That was top CID man in the county. And then? Apply for the job of assistant chief constable in another county? Very likely. He was certain, though, that he wouldn't run as easy an office as the Toff. When he was top man he would make them jump.

Brill was a small-town man. He would have felt uneasy in Birmingham or Manchester, let alone London. There was too much of it, too many villains, and some of them dead clever. Rawley was just right for him. He had pounded a beat there before transfer to the CID, and he really knew Rawley. He had driven around every bit of it, from the plush residential part where the business executives lived to the slums on the wrong side of the station. Brill shared two rooms and a sitting room with another sergeant, and his landlady liked having policemen in the house. It would do until he got a raise or found the right sort of girl to marry. But although Rawley was home ground, the country was another matter. Driving along these little roads which all looked to him the same, passing dead-and-alive villages which lacked even a fish-and-chip bar, he couldn't imagine how anybody in his senses wanted to live in them. The country was the sort of place where people would ride about on bicycles for twenty-two years.

The cottage was small and semidetached. There were rosebushes in the front garden; honeysuckle and winter jasmine climbed the walls. A man with a weather-beaten face was polishing an old Morris car in a driveway at the side of the cottage. He looked up as Brill approached, and said, "What can I do for you?" He spoke with a kind of burr that repelled the sergeant slightly. He was inclined to regard the standard urban accent of southern England as universal, and to deplore any departure from it as an affectation.

"Mr. Rogers? Brill, Rawley CID. Can I have a word with you?"

"Hold on just a minute. Looks beautiful, doesn't she? Nothing like real wax polish for protection." Brill, who regarded any car more than two years old as antique, nodded. Rogers led the way into the cottage, calling, "Mother, got a visitor."

In the next breath he said, "Mind your head." Too late. Brill's forehead had struck one of the blackened oak beams. Mrs. Rogers, large and smiling, expressed sorrow and went out to make a cup of tea. The room was comfortable if you liked that kind of room, with an inglenook fireplace, bits of brass on the walls mingling with family photographs. The armchair Brill sat in was comfortable but shabby.

"I thought you went round everywhere on a bicycle; didn't realize you had a car."

"That's right. I use the old bike for postal deliveries, never mind the weather. Mind you, I should have a van, but they wouldn't give me one, say it doesn't justify it. The car now, that's for our personal use. Bought her a year ago. Had a bit of trouble with her at first, but she's all right now. Makes all the difference, means we can get down to the sea any time we want to."

"Don't know how anyone lives without one here." Brill offered a cigarette, which was refused, lighted one himself. "Giluso; does that name mean anything to you? Abel Giluso, Batchsted Farm." When he saw the flare of alarm in the man's eyes he knew he was home.

"I don't think I know the name."

"You know Batchsted Farm, of course. Derelict, isn't it? How long since it was occupied?"

Rogers got up and turned away toward his wife, who was coming in the door with a tray containing tea and a cake. "He's asking how long since Batchsted Farm was occupied, Mother. About four years, wouldn't you say?"

The tray went down on the table with a clatter. Mrs. Rogers said something which might have been agreement. A cup of tea stood beside Brill, with a piece of cake.

"You knew nobody was living at the farm. Why did you deliver letters there?"

The postman's mouth opened and closed again. His wife said, "I told you."

Rogers found his voice. "It wasn't my business. The letters were addressed there, I put them in the box. Why shouldn't I?"

"Letters delivered to a place where there'd been nobody living for years and nobody could live because it was derelict," Brill said jeeringly. "Come on now, you're not that big a fool. You knew somebody was going to pick them up."

"You'd best tell him," the woman said. Rogers stayed silent. She went over to the mantel above the fireplace, lifted the lid off a blue china hen and took out an envelope. "He got this in the post."

The envelope was typed, and addressed to "Mr. Rogers, Postman," at his address. It was date-stamped "London, May 20." Inside was a slip of paper, also typed. It said:

Please deliver all mail for A. Giluso, Batchsted Farm, East Road, Sutton Willis, to box in front of house. Shall be moving in later this year. Many thanks for your trouble.

"There were two ten-pound notes came with it," she said. "That's a lot of money to us."

"She didn't want me to do it, but it was the car, you see." Rogers was apologetic. "It came in very handy, paid for the work on the car. She was laid up, needed a new cylinder head."

"I told him no. But he said there would be no harm."

Brill did not waste time on comment. "Have you had any other letters from him, received any more money?"

"No."

"How many letters have you put in the box? Think. It's important."

"I can't remember, not for certain. A dozen perhaps. Not many more."

"Did you notice the postmarks?"

"I think they were all London."

"And you're certain you never saw anyone picking them up?"

"Yes. Look, what's it all about? What's he been up to, this man?"

162

Mrs. Rogers said, "You don't have to report this to the head postmaster, do you? It might mean Ted loses his pension."

Her husband looked at Brill, and found no hope in his contemptuous stare. "You should never have told him, Mother, you should never have said about the money."

"I'll have to make a report." Brill put the envelope into his briefcase. "This may be important evidence in the Allbright murder." Mrs. Rogers gasped. "You should have stuck to your bicycle, Rogers. Cars are not for peasants."

Twenty thirty hours, Saturday evening. A fine evening, but clouds thickening and the sky growing dark. At just about the time that Brill was bumping his head on the Rogerses' oak beam, Hazleton was looking with approval at another country cottage. Or at least it was called a cottage, but Oakdene Cottage was a small and very pretty seventeenth-century red brick house, a couple of minutes' drive out of Crampton village. A thick hedge concealed it from the road, and a piece of well-kept grass lay outside the hedge, protected by white chains and bollards from the parking of cars. A short drive led past a large barn on the right and a scrupulously smooth lawn on the left up to the house. The effect was extremely neat. Hazleton liked it, as he liked the modern antique lantern hanging outside.

The balding man who came to the door acknowledged that he was Mr. Darling. Hazleton was shown into a living room where silver saltcellars and sugar sifters stood in one glass-fronted cabinet and pieces of china in another, newspapers were put tidily in a rack, and a little highly polished table stood beside every armchair. To the arm of one chair was fixed what is called a TV tray, with a space on it for a cup and another for a plate. Mr. Darling turned off the TV. Hazleton apologized for his intrusion.

"Not at all. I like to eat my supper watching the TV, but the programs get worse and worse, don't you think?"

"Can't say I get all that much time to watch, sir. My wife likes the quiz programs."

"Does she? Does she now?" Mr. Darling pondered on this,

then took the tray off the chair and called "Isabel" twice, the second time at the door. A tall thin woman with iron-gray hair came into the room.

"My sister Isabel. This is Chief Inspector Hazleton, isn't that right? Will you take any refreshment, Inspector?"

"Thank you, sir. A drop of whisky and water."

The gray-haired woman shook his hand. She had the beautiful clear skin of a child. "How do you do? Isn't it glorious weather? We can't complain about the summer, can we?"

"Glorious. You've got a lovely garden here. Looks a picture."

"A most beautiful summer. It makes me think about the past when the weather was so much finer, don't you think? But then everything about the past seems to me nicer than the present."

"Do you do the garden single-handed, ma'am? Or do you have help?"

"I beg your pardon?"

Mr. Darling, behind his sister, tapped his ear. Hazleton repeated the question more loudly. She gave a smile of great sweetness.

"I'm sorry. I am a little deaf; I daresay you have gathered that. Yes, I do the garden entirely on my own. Jonathan is—"

"I mow the lawn," her brother protested.

"He mows the lawn. But there is a great deal else to do in the garden, even to do to the lawn. It is too dark to see now, but I wish I could show you my herbaceous garden. The phlox are magnificent this year. Are you a keen gardener?"

Hazleton grinned. "I mow the lawn. That's if I can't get out of it."

She gave her sweet uncertain smile again. "I shall leave you men to your business. I hope you will come again in the daylight and look at my phlox."

When she had gone Darling said, "Isabel has been deaf for years. It's getting worse, but she won't admit it. She wears a hearing aid during the day, but as soon as I come home she puts it away. It can be trying at times, but she's a wonderful woman.

She keeps house for me here, runs this place entirely on her own. And does it very well."

"It's a lovely place," Hazleton said, and meant it. But it was time to cut the cackle. "You've got a property called Batchsted Farm on your books. Can you tell me about it?"

"I certainly can. You want to know why it's in its present state, I suppose."

"That among other things. Anything you can tell me."

"Very well. But you'll have to be prepared to sit back and listen for a couple of minutes. The last occupier was a man named Lionel Elliott, and the owner was Sir Lemuel Eames. Does that mean anything to you?" Hazleton shook his head. Darling chuckled. "No reason why it should. Sir Lemuel lived here in Crampton, though it was before my time, then went off to Ireland. They were a wealthy family—Eames the brewer, you know. Sir Lemuel was a bit of a rake, or had been in his time, and the story was that Lionel Elliott was his illegitimate son. He lived in the same house as a sort of poor relation while Sir Lemuel was here. The name of the one was Lemuel John Eames, and the other was Lionel John Elliott. Rather a coincidence, wasn't it? After Sir Lemuel went, Lionel stayed around and did all sorts of jobs—it was said that the old man made him an allowance. Then the arrangement was made by which Sir Lemuel let Lionel have Batchsted Farm, and do you know what he paid for it? Just ten pounds a year."

Hazleton stifled a yawn. This cool room in the prevailing heat made him conscious that he was very tired. "Neither of them is around now, I take it."

"They are in another place." There was something at once prim and jovial about Mr. Darling. "Lionel behaved like his father. He got a girl here pregnant, and went off to New Zealand. That was four and a half years ago, and Batchsted Farm has been empty ever since. First Sir Lemuel's attitude was that his tenant would come back—you understand, this fiction was always kept up. In the meantime he refused to have anything done to the place, because he said Lionel could carry out and pay for all the necessary work when he came back. Then about two years ago Lionel died in New Zealand in a boating accident. He had married out there, and left a baby son. Six months later Sir Lemuel died, of drink it was said. He made no will, and his nearest relative was a cousin. But in the meantime the Elliott family claimed that Lionel's son, whom he had named Lemuel, was the heir. They said they had documents to prove it. The case has been going on ever since. Nothing is decided. In the meantime the trustees are willing to sell Batchsted Farm, but not to spend a penny on it. You see the result. I am afraid I have tired you, Inspector."

Hazleton opened his eyes. "It's no wonder you can't sell the place. But still, it is on your books, and you do get people asking about it."

"We do. But very few bother to go out and look at the place after they have been told of its condition."

"You wouldn't happen to have a list of the people who have asked about the property in the past few months? Or know whether one of them was a man named Giluso?"

"I'm afraid there is no list, but I'm sure I should remember that name. The answer is no, Inspector."

"There's reason to think the name is assumed," Hazleton said gloomily. "He might have used another. Or he may not even have looked at the place."

"I've not been much help, I'm afraid. Perhaps if I knew the reason for your inquiries—if you'll forgive my curiosity."

"No reason why you shouldn't know, as long as you keep it to yourself. There's an old post box outside the property. We think it's been used as a letter drop by a man we'd like to talk to in relation to the Allbright murder."

"I see. Did you ever trace the French girl who disappeared a little earlier? Because I am afraid I may have been the unwitting means of putting you off the track."

"I don't follow." Hazleton looked at the estate agent with more interest than he had previously shown. Darling blinked at him.

"At just about the time she disappeared I reported that a girl who had worked for me was missing, a Miss Brown. I saw a very pleasant young man, his name was Plender, and I think he made inquiries. Then Miss Brown turned up a little later on. I think she'd just decided to go home without telling anybody— a most inconsiderate thing to do—and I expect inquiries about the other girl were stopped as well. That's what I meant by putting you off the track."

Hazleton remembered tearing a strip off Hurley about it. "You did right to report it. Though of course three-quarters of missing person reports turn out to be false alarms."

In the hall they passed Isabel, drifting in the direction of the stairs. Darling came out of the house with him. It was dark now, the night warm and thundery, the sky pricked with stars. There was a scent of honeysuckle. Hazleton drew in a breath.

"Lovely place you've got here. Peaceful."

"We've been here twenty years. It's a good deal changed since I bought it, I can tell you. That barn was pretty well a ruin, and the house itself was fairly tumbledown. Would you like to see the barn?"

Hazleton excused himself. He had had enough of Mr. Darling, who was amiable enough but impressed him as a considerable waster of time.

Twenty-one thirty hours, Saturday evening. Back at the station, Hazleton and Brill considered what they'd got after chasing up to London and around the countryside. It didn't seem to be all that much. They had found out how the man communicated with his victims—a plural which actually was not yet established—but they were no nearer associating him with Vane or anybody else, or finding out whether he had a female partner. Inquiries had been made about a car picking up a girl answering the description of Pamela Wilberforce in or near Station Road on Friday night, so far without result. Altogether, they knew a lot more, but it didn't seem to help very much. Brill

167

thought it was odd that nobody had seen the letters collected. The DCI disagreed.

"This Giluso or Lugosi or whatever his real name is has to be somebody who passed that way a couple of times a week, that's all. He stops his car in the lane, strolls along to the box. If somebody happens to come along—the lane's not used much— he turns his back on the road and looks over the fields. If not he opens the box, takes out his mail. Somebody with a car, probably somebody not tied to office hours. You can't even say that for sure, because the letters may have been picked up at night."

"Somebody who knew the postman Rogers."

"Or got his name on some excuse, which wouldn't have been difficult. Obviously he knows the locality, but we knew that already. That poor stupid sod."

"Who?"

"Rogers. He's most likely lost his pension, possibly his job, and for what? Twenty quid."

"He should have thought of that before he did it."

"Don't be such a bloody sanctimonious bastard, Sergeant." Hazleton contemplated the envelope and letter sent to Rogers as though they contained some magic property which would be revealed by scrutiny. This, or something like it, proved to be the case. He pulled out the file of cards from Bert Norman, and began to look through them, then pushed three of the cards over to Brill and said, "Look." His cheeks were shining, his always slightly bulging eyes looked likely to pop out.

Brill looked at the cards, which included the one for Giluso, and then at the envelope and note sent to Rogers. The top of the *l* in all the samples was very worn and al- most invisible, and both *s* and *t* were slightly out of align- ment. There could be little doubt that the index cards had been typed on the same machine as the envelope and note. Brill stared at them, dumbfounded.

"But that means—it must mean she knows Giluso."

"It means I want to talk to her." Hazleton drew the telephone to him and asked the operator to get hold of Detective Inspector Murch at East Dulwich. He had already fulfilled the needs of protocol by telling Murch of the visit they had paid to Westfield Grove. Now he asked the inspector to pick up Bert Norman at once.

Twenty-two thirty hours. The telephone rang. It was Murch. Bert Norman had packed and gone. She had taken all her clothes, and presumably the typewriter, since there was no sign of it.

Hazleton thanked the inspector, put down the telephone and cursed. They could and would try to trace her movements. They would no doubt find a taxi driver who had taken her to a railway station, and there the trail would probably end. Should he have taken her in that afternoon? There had been no obvious grounds for it, but it was in a state of dissatisfaction with the case and everything connected with it, including himself, that Hazleton went home and dropped into bed. It had been a hard Saturday.

23

Dead Sunday

▬ ▬ ▬ ▬ ▬ ▬ ▬ ▬ ▬ ▬ ▬ ▬ ▬ ▬ ▬ ▬ ▬ ▬ ▬

Sunday. In the best part of Rawley a day to mow the lawn, clip the hedge, weed the flower beds. A morning for golf or tennis, nine holes or a couple of sets, drinks in the clubhouse, then home to lunch. At eleven o'clock Paul Vane appeared at the tennis club, already, as Peter Ponsonby said, a little under the influence. He could not be deterred from playing in a mixed doubles, could hardly hit a ball, and halfway through the first set fell over and grazed his cheek. Peter took him home and talked about it afterward to a few appreciative friends.

"Really rather *grim*. You know his wife has left him? He told me that on the way back. He asked me in, and the place is really a bit of a shambles. He just doesn't know how to look after himself; I know of course some men don't, and can't bear to be alone. But then another thing is that he seems to have some sort of persecution mania. He said the police were trying to fix a crime on him that he'd never committed and that he'd never touched Louise—as though I'd suggested anything different. And he kept talking about how horrible dead bodies are. I mean, it was eerie. Go round and see him? Oh, I don't think I'd advise it. Do you know, when I said I wouldn't have a drink and suggested he might have had enough, he positively ordered me out of the house."

At lunchtime Paul rang up the Parkinsons. Alice talked to him, although her mother warned her not to do so. She put down the receiver after a few sentences. "Abuse," she said calmly. "Nothing but abuse and bad language. He was drunk. You'd think at this point he might try to exercise some measure of control."

"What did he say?" Norah Parkinson averted her head slightly, prepared for the worst.

"Just rubbish. Something about not being able to forget the smell of a dead body."

Her mother's eyes widened. "You don't suppose he really had something to do with that girl's death? What an awful thing if it were true. Just think what people would say."

In the afternoon Paul Vane slept. In the evening he started drinking again, opened a tin of luncheon meat and ate half of it, threw clothes into a suitcase for his visit to Grattingham Manor, and went on drinking.

He had been the subject of discussion at the conference held at County HQ on Sunday morning. Present: Sir Felton Dicksee, DCS Paling, DCI Hazleton. Paling was in favor of bringing Vane in again and interrogating him more thoroughly this time. He based himself on that original typewritten letter, repeating all the arguments he had used originally. He continued: "And that outing on Friday night when he deliberately shook off our man had some meaning, surely."

Hazleton disagreed. "It's true his movements on Friday night don't check out exactly, but they don't leave much time for killing and disposing of the Wilberforce girl. And who would Vane's partner be?"

Paling put his fingertips together. "What about his step-daughter, Jennifer?" Hazleton barely refrained from a contemptuous snort. "I see you don't think much of the idea, but she was the one who disposed of the typewriter, after all."

"A much better candidate would be this Bert Norman woman. She's obviously in it up to her neck."

Paling was enjoying this speculative wrangling, but Sir Felton listened with increasing irritation. Was it for this that he had given up a morning at the Athletic Club? "Action, gentlemen," he cried. "Less talk and more action. The Norman woman slipping through our hands—I don't like that. What's being done about her?"

"We're looking for a taxi driver who might have taken her as a fare, and her description's been circulated," Hazleton said stolidly. "London have found out a bit about her background. She's been at the address where we saw her for about two months, maybe a bit longer. She lived there alone according to the neighbors. Men came there occasionally, but they were presumably those who were placing or answering ads. She talked about one particular man named Alastair, but nobody seems to have noticed him. So perhaps she had no man friend, but wanted us to think she had." Sir Felton was about to interrupt, but Hazleton went remorselessly on. "Something else that's interesting. The magazine, *Meet Up*, had been going for several months. Previously it was sent out from an address in Mitcham. That's been checked, and it was an accommodation address, a general shop. The man there has been interviewed, and he says different boys used to come in and collect letters once a week."

"What's interesting about that?" Sir Felton asked.

"Just that the Norman woman's a recent importation. It looks as if she was a kind of manageress, not the person who really ran the thing."

"And where is she? And where's this man who did run the filthy magazine, if he exists?"

"I don't know, sir."

Sir Felton put his hands flat on the desk, and glared. He looked both ridiculous and ferocious. "The Allbright girl was murdered. The French girl was last seen in this district. So was the Wilberforce girl. I want a full-scale search for them both, Paling, and I want it mounted straightaway. Every available man, every possible means. Everybody working flat out, going at full pressure. No criticism of any individual, but it's something we should have done before. Agreed?"

Paling stifled a sigh. All this meant setting up a field HQ, directing things himself, being out of bed till all hours. He did not relish the prospect.

When Sally had a call from Sergeant Brill, saying that he would like to talk to her, she knew that she would have to tell her parents about Louise and Pamela and the letters. To her surprise they were more reproachful than angry, asking why she had not told them all about it earlier. Half an hour after she had told them, Brill arrived, and asked her dozens of questions, mostly about things she might have forgotten, like whether Louise had said anything precise about meeting the man who had advertised, and whether she could remember any particular phrases in the letter to Pamela. She did her best, but as she kept repeating, she had told the inspector everything she knew. She did not like Brill's manner, and she ended the interview in tears.

During the afternoon the laboratory reported on the typewriter used for the note to Rogers and the card index files. It was an Adler portable, not of the most recent kind.

A taxi driver had been found who had taken a woman answering to the description of Bert Norman from East Dulwich to Leicester Square Underground station. There the trail petered out.

In the late afternoon police search parties started to make a search of Batchsted Farm and the surrounding area, and also to look wider than they had done previously in relation to Planter's Place. Hazleton knew that such searches are not often successful unless you are looking in a specific area for something that is likely to be found there. However, it was the kind of operation he enjoyed, and he conducted it energetically. He kept in touch with Paling by telephone, which seemed all that was necessary at this stage.

During the afternoon, also, Brian Hartford went to see his wife. He found her much better than usual. She was lucid, seemed perfectly normal, and pleaded with him to let her come home. These were the worst times because, as he knew from the past, the improvement would not be maintained. Making promises that could never be fulfilled was agony for him, but still he made them. Later he saw the doctor, who said that recently she had been worse than usual, talking about men who climbed the wall by suckers attached to their legs, and got into her room.

Afterward he met two American businessmen for drinks at their hotel. They represented the group that was interested in gaining control of Timbals, and it was understood that if they succeeded, Hartford would replace Lowson. On this basis he had given them a good deal of information which they could not have obtained otherwise, except by planting a man in the firm. The meeting was not satisfactory. There was a good deal of drinking, which Hartford disliked, and a lot of talk about the financial basis of a takeover and about the need to cut out dead wood. All of it was vague, and Joey Fiddick, the chief American representative, showed some fancy evasive footwork when he was asked about points of detail. Hartford went home feeling uneasy.

Among the routine operations to be undertaken during the search was the dragging and draining of the pond at Batchsted Farm. This proved, however, not to be a simple affair, because the pond was one of three connected to a spring. It was extremely deep, and special dredging equipment was needed. It was inevitable, of course, that Sir Felton should arrive just at the time that the ordinary dragging nets had proved to be useless. He sat on a shooting stick looking grimly at what was being done, then went to talk to Hazleton, who was established in a motorized trailer.

"You're going to need divers."

"Oh, I don't think so, sir. It's only a pond, after all, though it's very deep. I'm on to the dredging people now, but it's Sunday. They'll have the machine here in the morning."

"Let me have that telephone." Sir Felton started barking into it like a dog, slowly thawed into something like geniality. "First thing in the morning," he announced when he had put it down.

Diplomacy was not the DCI's strong point, but he managed to refrain from comment. Sir Felton was annoyed to find that Paling was not on the scene, but just then the DCS turned up. He had decided that he must tear himself away from the Roman coins at least to the extent of visiting the area. He went off with the chief constable to Planter's Place, where they watched men beating a way desultorily through fields, and poking about in ditches.

At eight-thirty it was becoming dark. Nothing had been discovered. Sir Felton had gone home long since, to swing on the parallel bars in his personal gym. Paling had returned to his coins, and to a new catalogue with some very desirable things in it. Hazleton called it off for the day.

Yet that was not the end of dead Sunday. It was a day which provided Ray Gordon with the first, and in fact the only, scoop of his life. He had taken a girl named Nita Lines on a mild variety of pub crawl, which ended at the Duke's Children. She did not refuse when he suggested that they should go up onto Green Common afterward. He parked the car, took a rug from the trunk, and they started to walk. Green Common belied its name, since part of it was a wood. They had reached the outskirts of the wood when Nita stumbled and fell. He picked her up.

"Oh, Ray," she said. "I fell over something. Soft and horrible."

"Never mind, let's go on."

"I couldn't, till I know what it is. I just couldn't."

He cursed under his breath, and drew out his lighter. It illuminated branches and green leaves. He started to say there was nothing, then stopped. Where she had fallen the leaves had shifted, and the lighter showed the decayed flesh of a hand and arm. At the same time he became aware of a most unpleasant smell.

He took the girl back to the car, drove off and found a telephone box. The time was twenty-three hours fifteen minutes.

Then all the telephones began to ring.

24

Extracts from a Journal

━━ ━━ ━━ ━━ ━━ ━━ ━━ ━━ ━━ ━━ ━━ ━━ ━━ ━━

Crisis. I feel that this is in every way a time of crisis in my life. I am separated from what I was. What I shall be, what I am *becoming*, is not yet.

This is typified in many things. Item. In Bonnie. She is necessary, or she has been necessary, but she now disgusts me. Her motives are the lowest—the lust for blood, the hankering after sex. When she sticks things up them, when she cuts and slices and tears, it is all a revenge on her parents. She told me that her father used to beat wickedness out of her, that her uncle put his thing into her mother and that she saw it. True or not? It is what she says. She had to be home by ten every evening. One night when her father found her with a boy he threatened the boy with an air gun, then beat her with a strap. True? I think she believes it.

She is not a proper participant in what should be sacred rites.

Item. *I am no longer Dracula.* The Count is dead, he belongs to the past. It is as though the stake had been driven through his heart. There is a season of horror films on TV. Last night I watched *Dr. Jekyll and Mr. Hyde*, not the 1941 film with Spencer Tracy, but Rouben Mamoulian's film in which handsome Jekyll can be seen slowly, slowly changing before our eyes to savage shaggy Hyde. I had seen it before, it is wonderful in the way that Hyde exults in his freedom, but last night I watched unmoved. And there are other films I have seen too—*Dr. Terror's House of Horrors* and Tod Browning's *Freaks*. Oh yes, I cried out when I saw that for the first time; oh yes, these freaks are my friends, I know them. They do not cause a flicker of excitement in me now.

Why is this? It is because I am approaching a new truth, a new purity. Long ago I copied out of the Master's work these words: "Everything that is deep, loves the mask. The deepest things of all have even a hatred of image and likeness. Is not the *opposite* the right cloak in which the nakedness of a God should go about?" I have always thought these words were the deepest, greatest truth. I have always worn the cloak of the opposite. But when the mask has been dropped, when you face the reality of the Will to Power, what then? Why, then your whole life is changed. You must have Power, you must dominate, and to do so you must be what the world calls cruel. But if you could, you would be merciful. If you could, you would love.

The masks of my life are slipping away. What is my true face?

Practical Comments. With the police visit to East Dulwich it was obvious that the magazine must end. It is little more than a year since it began, and I sent youths to that small shop in a Mitcham back street. At first I could not believe it when they came back carrying armfuls of letters from those moved by the frantic itch. Was this what people hid behind their different, discreet masks? I had not known it. So what had been begun for money, as an idea that occurred to me when I bought one of these magazines and answered an advertisement, became something else. I suppose there was an attraction in the magazine from the first, an attraction beyond money. Perhaps the idea of my own anonymity, of disguise? I cannot be sure. Not for months did I think that my mask, Dracula, who longed to rule and be loved, might find his worshipers here.

I read all this over. What does it tell me about the truth of masks? I do not know. What do I want? I do not understand. What are these things I have done or not done, what made me do them? I cannot be sure. My purpose is to understand the nature of reality, yet how strangely has it been made manifest.

Last night a dream. Creatures crying out, asking for pity. In a motorboat my fingers trailing through the sea. The sea was blood.

25

Sunday Night

▄▄ ▄▄ ▄▄ ▄▄ ▄▄ ▄▄ ▄▄ ▄▄ ▄▄ ▄▄ ▄▄ ▄▄ ▄▄ ▄▄ ▄▄ ▄▄ ▄▄

Just before midnight on Sunday the weather broke. The first drops of rain fell, warm, heavy, slow. In ten minutes these drops had become a steady downpour which soaked everything and everybody involved in the scene at Green Common—everything, that is, except the body, which was protected by a covering quickly rigged up on poles by the scene-of-crime squad, as soon as they got there.

Even so the body got wet, and the surrounding area became muddy although it had been roped off. And everybody else became very wet indeed—Hazleton directing affairs from his trailer after the first ten minutes; Paling wandering about with his hands in the pockets of his well-cut raincoat; Sir Felton Dicksee in sou'wester hat and thigh boots; Plender, who had come on duty just before Ray Gordon's telephone call to the police. And of course the scene-of-crime squad and their uniformed cousins, taking flashlight pictures, shouting incomprehensibly technical instructions, or just poking about in the surrounding grass, got wettest of all. Dozens of lights illuminated the dripping leaves and sodden ground and the driving lances of rain, some from the headlights of the police cars drawn up around, others from the floodlights set up by the scene-of-crime men.

Paling turned away after looking at the body, and almost bumped into Sir Felton. The chief constable was in an excited state. "Didn't I say it? Didn't I ask for a full-scale search? You see the results, Paling."

Paling felt damp soaking through his trousers, and he had had enough of the chief constable. "We weren't searching here, sir. Somebody stumbled over the body."

Sir Felton ignored this. "Who is she?"

"Not the Wilberforce girl. We'll know more when Dr. Otterley arrives. I don't know if Hazleton's got anything fresh."

Hazleton was on the telephone, and he was shouting. "Bloody well find him, and get him out here." He lowered his voice and said sweetly, "Tell Dr. Otterley I'm sorry to disturb him, but this is very urgent. Yes, I know you say he's out and you're trying to get a message through, my dear; I'm just saying this in case you talk to him." He put down the telephone. "Bloody doctors; what do we pay them for? It's Otterley, sir. His housekeeper says he's out somewhere at dinner, and can't be located. I believe he's tucked up in bed and she won't wake him up."

Sir Felton frowned. He never liked to hear even a hint of slackness. "Who is she, Hazleton?"

"We haven't disturbed the body, sir, but it's obvious she's been dead some time. It isn't the Wilberforce girl, but it could be the au pair. And she hasn't been where she is now for long; you can tell that from the state of the grass. Dumped in the past week, more recently very like. Covered by some sort of sacking bag, the kind you use for vegetables. Some clothes are there too, put beside her. Otherwise she's naked, as you may have seen."

"That gap in Vane's alibi," Paling said. He reminded the chief constable. "He went to a pub by Green Common on Friday night, then there was a time lag. Just about enough time to allow for dumping a body."

"Why should he do that?"

"We'd been talking to him, he got worried. Why do people do silly things?"

Hazleton did not want to disagree openly. He remained silent. There was a clatter outside. It was the mobile canteen, with cups of tea. Sir Felton took a silver-covered flask from his hip pocket, poured some of the contents into his plastic container of tea and offered it to his companions. Both accepted. Hazleton was thinking that there was something, after all, to be said for the chief constable, when he said sharply, "Poky place, this. Should have a proper murder room."

"Yes, sir. We didn't get the news until nearly eleven-thirty; too late to set up in a church hall or women's institute. With this we're right on the spot."

Sir Felton grunted. "Talked to the people who found the body? That journalist."

"Sergeant Plender's doing that now, sir. In one of the cars."

Plender talked first to Ray Gordon, then to the girl. There seemed no reason to suspect their stories of being untrue. Gordon had been mixed up in the case at an early stage, but why should he use this means of calling attention to himself? He had telephoned the London papers already, and was frantically anxious to ring them again.

"In a detective story you'd have arranged to find the body so that you could get a news scoop."

"If you believe that—"

Plender stopped him. "I don't. Just thought I'd mention it, that's all. Okay, we'll get your statement typed up and you can go."

Afterward Plender stretched luxuriously. He had brought himself up to date with what had been happening when he came on duty, and something in the reports he read had stirred his memory, although he could not think what it was. He decided to have another look through the papers in the morning.

182

Outside it rained, and they waited for the pathologist. Much police work, like other forms of coordinated effort, consists of waiting for something to happen, for some link in the chain of causation without which the whole thing is ineffective. In the meantime, however, the reports of the scene-of-crime men gave Paling and Hazleton something to think about. The clothes found beside the body were similar to those that Anne Marie Dupont had been wearing when she disappeared. Without moving the body it was possible to see a tarnished silver ring on the middle finger of her right hand, and Anne Marie had worn a similar ring. There would have to be a formal identification, but there seemed little doubt that the body was that of the missing au pair. All this was interesting for the DCS and the DCI (the CC, to their relief, had gone home), but those outside the trailer simply stood around and got wetter. They had been doing this for half an hour when Otterley arrived. It turned out that he had gone on from his dinner party to a friend's house for a nightcap. He was in the medical tradition of genial callousness.

"Well, what have you got for me? Something juicy, I hope." When he bent down beside the body he sniffed, and whistled. "Very gamy. Been hung too long, like pheasant. Some more light here, if you please. Why do people always find these things at night? Now, what's been happening to you, young lady? Nothing nice, by the look of it."

He opened his bag, took out a pair of forceps and some buff envelopes, carefully picked crumbs of something from the girl's body and put them in an envelope.

Half an hour later he reported to Paling and Hazleton. "You want me to perform miracles for you, gentlemen, no doubt. Too late at night for miracles, but actually there's nothing too difficult here. You'll understand I mean it's not difficult to make informed guesses. Facts will have to wait for the PM. Is that what you want?" They said it was.

"Right. She was a well-developed girl, good physical condition, height about five three, age about twenty. Cause of death strangulation. Some form of ligature, probably a rope—I'd better say again that these are guesses. She'd been physically assaulted, cuts all over her body, face, breasts, buttocks, genitals. What look like nasty bite marks on breasts and neck."

"Dracula," Hazleton said.

"What's that?"

"Nothing. Go on."

"Sexual assault too, again savage, brutal. May have been some sort of instrument. Looks as though her wrists were bound. The assaults weren't the cause of death though; that was the ligature. Just torture. Very jolly."

"Would you say one person was involved or two?" Paling asked.

"Two or three you mean, don't you?" Otterley replied with insolent good humor. "The victim was involved, very much so. How many others? Shouldn't care to say, may have been a dozen. PM may help, but I doubt it."

"When was she killed?"

"Not asking for the day and hour, I hope. Six weeks to two months ago. It's a guess, mind, but you'll find I'm right. Does it fit? From the looks on your faces I should say it does."

"It fits," Hazleton said. Anne Marie had disappeared on the night of May 27, and it was now the twenty-fifth of July.

"Of course you'd realized that she wasn't killed where she was found. Hasn't been there more than three days. But here's something you won't know. There are fragments of stuff in her hair, on her body, on that sack covering her. The lab will check on them, but they look to me like concrete not properly set."

"You mean she was buried in concrete and taken out again?"

"I must say that's the thought roaming about my mind. And now, gentlemen, I propose to depart for my bed and some well-earned shut-eye. I'll tell you more when I've had the lady on the slab, but don't expect anything dramatic. My guess would be that I've given you all the news that matters."

After Otterley's departure the scene rapidly changed, so that it resembled the dismantling of a big top after the end of a circus. The body was removed, the floodlights packed up, the improvised covering for the area around the body removed. The cars departed. There remained only the ropes surrounding the place where the girl had been found, and a solitary police car with a couple of men in it whose job was to keep away the curious.

Paling and Hazleton were among the last to leave. Should they pull in Vane for questioning, or leave him to stew until they got the lab report?

"I hate to say it at this time of night, but we ought to pick him up now," Paling said. "If he carried a body in his car boot there must be traces of it."

"And tomorrow he's going on some sort of management course in Hampshire."

They sent Plender to pick up Vane, and returned to Rawley. Twenty minutes later the sergeant rang to say that he could get no answer from the house, and that Vane's car was not in the garage.

"Our bird's flown," Paling said. "That settles it. We pull him in."

Hazleton agreed. It looked as though his sense of smell had failed him after all.

Hazleton dropped into bed at a quarter to four in the morning. At eight-thirty the telephone rang and rang. Plender's voice, fresh and cheerful (but then he had had time off), said, "The dredger's found another one, sir."

The DCI was still half asleep. "Another what?"

"Body. In the pond at Batchsted Farm. The Wilberforce girl."

26

One Way of Solving Your Problems

Monday morning, 0 nine thirty hours. Paul Vane drove his car up an avenue of oak trees which led to an eighteenth-century country house with a lot of later additions that had converted its original squareness into a rectangle. A man took his suitcase and directed him to the garages at the back. When he returned the door was opened by a well-scrubbed smiling figure dressed in country tweeds.

"I'm Jay Burns Lawrence. I'd like it if you'd call me Jay. And you're . . ."

"Paul Vane."

"Glad to know you, Paul." He led the way through a paneled hall to a large comfortable living room where two men sat talking. "This is Paul Vane. Paul, meet Peter Madeley and Geoffrey Sturtevant-Evans." Madeley was tall, with a craggy face and deep-set eyes, Sturtevant-Evans a dapper figure who had an air of wishing to dissociate himself from his companions and surroundings.

"You're bright and early," Lawrence said.

"I drove down last night and stayed at the pub in the village."

Lawrence smacked his thigh. "If only I'd known. You could have stayed here, like Peter and Geoffrey. Of course they had some way to drive."

"From Leeds." Madeley made it sound like Vladivostok.

"And Geoffrey comes from Swansea. They wanted to be in at the start of things, like yourself. The others will be along later; quite a small party this time, eight in all. Smoke, Paul?"

The cigarette case opened like a trap. "No, thanks."

"I'll say to you what I've already said to the others. You're here for a couple of weeks. You'll find mealtimes posted in your rooms, and we'd like you to be here for them, but apart from that you'll do what you like for the first week. Get to know each other, discuss any problems you may have, either business or personal, play games—there are tennis courts, though I'm afraid the weather's not too good for them; a very well fitted games room—go out for walks, do whatever you like."

"Church architecture is one of my interests," Madeley said sepulchrally.

"I believe Grattingham Church has a rather famous font. By the end of the week you'll be tuned in both to yourselves and to each other. In week two you're split into groups of four—actually, you'll find you split naturally into groups—and you carry out certain practical work situation assignments. I won't go into them in detail. I'll say no more than this. The course fulfills the old religious injunction: Know thyself. And it fulfills another: Know thy neighbor."

Later Paul Vane was shown up to a light, airy bedroom, with a window looking out onto the garages at the back and the parklike gardens. He stared at his face in the mirror. There were deep dark shadows under his eyes; the graze on his face showed clearly. He breathed on his hand and sniffed. It seemed to him that a whiff of liquor came off. "I shall have to be very careful," he said, without having any idea of what he meant.

Outside a thin rain persistently fell.

Monday morning. Ten hours fifteen minutes. A thin rain persistently fell. They had opened up Batchsted Farm and taken the body of Pamela Wilberforce inside. Dr. Otterley, jokier than ever this morning, had made his preliminary examination. The girl had probably been killed on Friday night, possible early on Saturday morning. She had been strangled with a ligature like the others, cut like the others. Her genitals and rectum had been violated by some sort of instrument like a bottle or a dildo. In this case, however, there were no bite marks on breast and neck, and there had been no attempt at intercourse. More detailed news after the postmortem. "Keeping me busy," Otterley said with a chuckle as he drove away. "Try and wait twenty-four hours before you find the next one, there's a good chap."

A murder room had been set up in the village hall at Sutton Willis. There Hazleton and a depressed Paling dealt with the mass of incidental details like getting hold of Pamela's father to identify his daughter, and Dick Service to identify Anne Marie. Ray Gordon's telephone calls had caught the morning papers, which blossomed into headlines ranging from MISSING GIRL FOUND DEAD IN WOOD to RAWLEY MANIAC STRIKES AGAIN. The London reporters were down in force, and discovery of the second body had made them frantic as bees in search of their queen. Paling felt that he could hardly bear it, and the fact that the chief constable might arrive at any time did nothing to assuage that feeling. He made a statement to the reporters suggesting that an early arrest was likely. This sent most of them to the village pub, which opened at ten thirty to better business than it had done for years.

Monday morning, ten thirty hours. Plender stood at the door of Bay Trees fiddling with the lock. DC Paterson waited behind him. Plender had had no time to look at the papers and check on that curious feeling about missing something. The second key worked, and they stepped into the hall.

There is something unmistakable about an empty house, and Plender knew that there was nobody in it even as he called Vane's name. They searched methodically from top floor to cellar, finding nothing of interest until they reached the cellar.

The floor here was concrete, but in one corner this had been disturbed, and an excavation made. It was obviously the place from which Anne Marie Dupont's body had been taken.

The light in the cellar was dim. Paterson shone a flashlight at Plender's direction. He saw that the concrete near the part dug up was of a lighter color, and different in texture, from the rest of the cellar floor.

"He buried her and concreted it over," Paterson suggested.

"Yes. But why dig her up?"

Paterson was not hesitant about expressing his opinions. "This hole where he put her, Sarge, it's not very deep. You can see that from the amount of soil there now. I reckon he did the job in a hurry, didn't put her far enough down, spread the concrete thin and uneven, and it cracked. Then she'd start to smell."

"I think you've got something. Though what was to stop him doing some more digging and making a proper job of it the second time? Odd, isn't it?"

Paterson had run out of ideas.

Otterley had done the PM on the French girl, which for the most part confirmed what they already knew. The fragments adhering to her hair and body were concrete mixed with earth and sand. The only fresh point of interest was the likelihood that the girl had had sexual relations shortly before her death. When Plender rang to report what he had found, Paling exploded with irritation.

"He smelled trouble and he's on the run. If we'd taken him a few hours earlier—"

Hazleton looked up from the PM details. "He just might have gone to the place he said he was going, Grattingham Manor." He gave the number to the girl on the improvised switchboard. "Ask for Mr. Lawrence. Don't say who's calling."

When he put down the telephone five minutes later he refrained from looking at his superior. "He's there. Stayed the night at some pub in the village, came early this morning. I've asked Lawrence to let us know if he makes any attempt to leave."

"It's no more than a two-hour drive. I'll take him myself." Paling felt that his nerves this morning simply would not stand a session with the chief constable.

"It's Tubby Mouncer's patch and he used to be a mate of mine. Shall I have a word with him?"

Paling agreed. Protocol must be observed. He listened without pleasure to the DCI's hearty conversation with Detective Chief Inspector Mouncer, of the Hampshire CID, who promised to be at Grattingham Manor in person, and then got away. As he went down the lane, accompanied by Brill and a driver, he passed Sir Felton's Jaguar.

An elegant young man named Gray had arrived. He was talking to Sturtevant-Evans.

"When were you up?"

"Sixty-three. At the House. And you?"

"New College. You must know old Puffy Spokes."

"Of course. And that ghastly little cockney who used to go round with him." Sturtevant-Evans squeaked, in a caricature of a cockney accent, " 'Ow's it goin', then, mate?' What was his name?"

"What *was* his name? Barber?"

"No, some other pleb occupation. Taylor?"

Paul Vane threw back his head and closed his eyes. He could feel his left arm twitching. The voices went on, chattering like birds. He felt his arm move, apparently of its own volition, so that it was raised like a semaphore. When he opened his eyes the arm lay harmlessly on his chair. He got to his feet and walked hurriedly out of the room. The door opened and closed after him. It was Madeley.

"There's another sitting room, you know." He led the way across the hall. This second sitting room had magazines on tables and in racks, like a blend of doctor's waiting room and a public library. Madeley sat in an armchair beside Paul Vane. "I gather you don't care for those university types. I don't get on with them myself. I'm not English, you know, I was brought up in the Welsh valleys. Can you tell the accent? I've tried to get rid of it." He spoke as if it were bad breath.

"I wouldn't have known."

"It's good of you to say so. The English don't like the Welsh, you know. It's held me back. What's your trouble?"

"How do you mean?" He shrank away slightly. Madeley leaned closer.

"We're all here because there's something wrong with us. I'll tell you what it is with me. I'm production manager at Swan Building; that's an important job, mind. I've got two of these university types to deal with now. They despise me, I can tell it."

"And that's why you're here?"

"They say the production graph's been falling," Madeley said darkly. "They talk about loss of concentration. It's an excuse. What about you?"

"I'm just here for a refresher course. New techniques of handling people, motivational research, that kind of thing."

"They tell you that. You'll find there's more to it, there's something hidden."

The door opened, and Lawrence's well-brushed head appeared around it. He said with relief, "There you are. Getting together, fine. Another couple of guests are here—"

Vane brushed past him without speaking, and ran up the wide staircase. Lawrence stood at the bottom of it until he heard a door close.

In his bedroom Paul Vane took out a writing pad from his suitcase, sat at a desk looking out onto the old stables converted into garages, with beyond them the dripping trees, and began to write.

Brill had heard about Paling's weakness, or perhaps it was strength, for theorizing about a case, and was prepared to play

191

up to it. "You're sure about Vane, then, sir? There's no doubt he's chummy?"

Paling disliked these colloquial expressions, but at the same time welcomed the chance to test again the links in the chain that bound Vane to the murders. There was his background as a sex offender, although one never actually charged, and the conjectural impotence which often marked sex killers. And then there was the evidence: the use of his typewriter, his behavior on Friday night, and of course the fact that Anne Marie's body had been in his cellar.

"It's not watertight, mind you. But it's good enough to charge him. I don't doubt we shall find traces of concrete in his car boot."

"Yes, sir. Of course we haven't found any link between him and the sex mag or the woman who ran it. Or the woman he mentioned in that letter."

"It's perfectly possible, Sergeant, and I think likely, that the woman in the letter doesn't exist."

"Chummy was on his owneo."

"Vane operated alone, yes."

"And when you say the body was in his cellar, sir, it wasn't his cellar then. What I mean is, he hadn't moved in when the French girl was killed. Why should he plant a body in what was going to be his own cellar; why not get rid of it at once?"

"That's something we can't know. My guess would be that he kept it there because he didn't want it to be found at all. I've made a study of this sort of killer, and they often do keep bodies around. Think of Christie, think of Crippen. Then when things got too hot Vane decided to dump it."

Brill did not carry the argument beyond this point, for fear of upsetting his superior. His own belief was that Vane had done it, but that the case against him was full of holes.

Monday, twelve thirty hours. Plender had the file of the case, or rather the cases, in the middle of his desk, and a tray of coffee and sandwiches on the left-hand side. The file went back to the beginning, the disappearance of Anne Marie, and included everything—interviews, reports of conversations, phony confessions, everything that had happened up to Sunday night. He ate and drank as he went systematically through the file to find what it was that made his memory itch.

Monday, twelve thirty hours. They had met Tubby Mouncer, who was naturally enough the kind of big jolly man that Paling most disliked, at County HQ. Paling filled him in on the details as they drove out to Grattingham Manor. Protocol, again, demanded that the local force should be present at the arrest.

The door of the manor opened almost before they had drawn up their cars. Jay Burns Lawrence welcomed them into the hall.

"I suppose there's no use in saying I hope it isn't serious, because if it wasn't you wouldn't be here. But I know you'll be as discreet as possible. I thought Vane seemed a little distracted, I must say."

"Where is he now?"

"In his room. Shall I call him?"

"Not yet. First of all we want to see his car."

Paul Vane had finished his writing long ago. He had been sitting holding his head in both hands, and staring out at the rain. He watched the three men pick their way across the puddles in the courtyard, get to his car where it stood under cover and open the trunk. One of the men took out a flashlight and shone it inside the trunk, another went around and opened the car door.

Paul Vane folded the pages he had written, added two sentences, put them in an envelope, carefully gummed it down at the back, wrote three words on the front. Then he got up from the writing table.

It did not need a microscope to see the traces of dirt and

concrete in the boot. There was a smell like that of rotting vegetables. A torn piece of sacking that looked as if it would match the sacking beside the body had caught on a screw. There were what might have been fragments of decayed flesh. They looked inside the car for bloodstains or other marks which might indicate that one or more of the girls had been in it, but they found nothing. Mouncer raised his eyebrows and Paling nodded.

Lawrence was waiting in the hall, a little anxious. He started to say something. Mouncer patted him on the shoulder.

"Just you don't worry, lad, and nobody'll get hurt. Which is his room?"

"I'll show you." As they went up the staircase two men came out of another room into the hall, and stared at them with frank curiosity. "Do please be discreet."

"The sooner we start the sooner we'll be away. This one, is it?" Mouncer turned the handle gently, knocked. There was no reply. Paling whispered to Lawrence, "Call him."

Lawrence said in a shaky voice, "Could I have a word with you, Paul?" Silence.

Mouncer said to Lawrence, "Have you got a key?" He did not bother to keep his voice down.

"In the office downstairs. But if there's a key inside you can't—"

"We'll manage. Get it."

When Lawrence came back, Mouncer took the key, dropped to his knees and fiddled with the lock. There was the sound of the key inside dropping to the floor. He put in the other key and turned it. The door opened. They went in.

The room was empty, or it appeared empty. It was Brill who saw the figure hanging behind the door, its face red, and swollen like that of a sufferer from bad toothache, a gaudy tie making a noose around the neck. They got him to the floor, took off the tie, Mouncer and Brill began to work on him. Paling stood aside with a look of distaste. Jay Burns Lawrence said, "Good God," and kept repeating it.

"Shut the door," Paling said.

Lawrence shut the door. He continued to stare at the body on the floor, shaking his head like a swimmer coming up after a dive. "Hanged himself. I'd never have believed it."

"Don't stand there, man. Ring for a doctor."

Lawrence went out, still shaking his head. Paling went to the window, looked out. "He saw us by the car." He picked up the envelope, which was addressed "To the police," opened it.

Brill said, "No good," and rested back on his heels. Mouncer still worked away. Paling read what Vane had written.

I am writing this because in these last three months, since we moved to Rawley, my life has been ruined. Alice has left me. I have been sent to this extraordinary house on a kind of schoolboy training course, and I know that when I return Hartford is going to get me sacked. The police obviously suspect me of murder. My life as I know it is at an end. Can I start a new one? I don't think so.

But I want to put the record straight. I did one stupid thing, and I lied to the police, but I have committed no crime. *Somebody has been persecuting me.*

I now put down all I know about the Allbright case. (I suppose you might call it a statement for the police, but I shall probably never give it to them, I shall probably tear it up.) I told the absolute truth in my first statement. I hardly knew Louise Allbright. I took her home and kissed her, nothing more. When the police found out about the other girls, they suspected me, but they were wrong. I know nothing about the letter done on my typewriter. I cannot explain it. I told the absolute truth about everything.

Until Friday night.

On Friday I came home, and Alice had gone. I had some drinks, went over the house and down into the cellar to see if she had taken her suitcases. She had. There was a space where they had stood, and the concrete there was cracked and broken. There was also a bad smell. I pushed away some of the broken concrete and found a body.

Who was it, how long had it been there, how did it get there? I have no idea. But I was frightened. I felt that I must get rid of it. I was being watched, there was a police car outside. I thought they would come in, find this body and arrest me.

I got a spade, dug it out—the grave was very shallow, and the concreting over had been badly done. I put it in the car boot, with a sack over it and some clothes which were in the grave. I went to Green Common, parked there, put it down covered with the sacking, and covered it with leaves and branches.

It was a woman. I had nothing to do with her death.

So far she has not been found, but of course she will be, very soon. Then they will ask more questions. I can't stand that.

Why has this happened to me?

Paul Vane

At the bottom a few more words were scrawled:

The police are here now, looking at the car. I can't go through any more.

Mouncer stood up, wiped his forehead. "He's had his last meal, that's for sure. Got a nice little confession there, to make it all neat?"

"No confession."

"But he did it all right. Or why string himself up? Nice tie too."

Paling looked down at the figure on the floor. "I don't know."

Brill looked down too. "It's one way of solving your problems," he said.

Monday, twelve thirty hours. Bob Lowson beamed at Brian Hartford.

"Sit down, Brian. Glad you could spare a minute. I thought you'd like to know that Joey Fiddick is out. The group's no longer interested. Or rather we've done a deal with them by which we get access to American outlets. We're going into the States in a big way. It's going to cost money, mind you, but it's a good deal. It's not what you had in mind."

196

Denial would have been pointless. "No."

"It brings your position into question." Hartford thought he knew what was coming, but he was wrong. On the principle that a victor can afford to make concessions, Lowson suggested a shift and extension of Hartford's empire, to include overall control of the new American setup. He accepted immediately.

Sometimes it is a good idea to crush rebels, but often it is better to buy them. Bob Lowson was so pleased with himself that he rang and made an appointment with Dr. Winstanley.

Monday, fourteen thirty hours. Hazleton entered Plender's office, slammed the door behind him. He looked as dangerous as a wild boar. "You've heard?"

"What's that?"

"Vane saw them looking at his car, hanged himself. Shouldn't happen, that kind of thing. Bloody stupid."

"He did it?" Plender sounded disappointed.

"He left a statement, admitted nothing except getting rid of the French girl's body. Says he found her in the cellar and got the wind up." He noticed the pile of papers in front of the sergeant. "What the hell have you got there?"

"It's the file. I knew there was some word or phrase I'd read which meant something; it had been used by somebody in the case before."

"I don't know what you're talking about."

Plender swallowed before he spoke. Hazleton realized that he was very excited. "Brill put in a very full report of your interview with Alberta Norman. Here's one thing she said about this Alastair she talked about. 'He was a layabout. And a pinchfist too.' Did she say that?"

"Very likely. Why?"

"It's an unusual word, 'pinchfist,' don't you agree?"

"What of it, Plender? It's quite probable she invented this Alastair man as a cover-up for something else. Come to the point, if there is one."

"Here's a report I made on the questioning of a woman named Joan Brown. When I asked her why she left her job, she said the man was an old pinchfist." He pointed out the line. "Isn't it remarkable that she should use the same word? What did this Norman woman look like, sir? No, let me tell you. Five two or three, rather dumpy, high forehead, nose with a bit of a droop at the tip"—he sketched it—"rather thick legs, rather big feet."

"That nose is right. And you mean the frizzy hair and the makeup and glasses—"

"Plain glass in them. Those were the things she could alter. The nose she couldn't. I wish I hadn't been off that afternoon. I'd have recognized her."

Hazleton took the sheet on which Plender had put down his interview with Joan Brown, and read it. He remained unexcited. "It sounds as though you may be right. Does it help? Joan Brown disappeared and turned up again, but what then?"

"You'll see in this report she says she'd gone to her parents. I didn't ring them then because there seemed no point. I called them today, talked to them both. Her mother said Joan came home in a state of collapse, screaming and crying that she'd done something terrible. Within a week she'd got over it and they started having rows, which I gather was as usual. The rows went on till she upped and left. She'd never got on with her parents since she was twelve and stopped going to church. They're both strict Methodists; they spout hell-fire and damnation even down the phone."

"Have they heard of her since?"

"Yes. In the last month they've had two registered envelopes, each with fifty quid in it. No letter inside, just a note that said 'Love, Joan.' Another thing. When she was fourteen she got into trouble. She caught a dog, tied it up, cut it all over till it bled to death." Hazleton stared at him. "She got very unpopular in the district after that, left as soon as she was out of school. They've only seen her occasionally since then."

"You think she took part in killing the French girl, got frightened and ran home, then decided she liked it and came back."

"It makes sense, sir, doesn't it? Especially when you think about the dog."

Hazleton agreed. "It makes sense. It's all theory, mind you. The DCS would love it."

Plender coughed apologetically. "That's not all, sir."

"More theories? You don't want to do too much fancy thinking, Harry. Gives you piles, keeping your arse glued too long to a chair."

"This isn't theory. I've taken it over to the lab and they've checked it out. I happened to notice it going through the file." He tried to speak with becoming modesty. He put on the table the note typed to the postman Rogers and its accompanying envelope, then put beside it the estate agent's typed particulars of Planter's Place. The particulars had been issued by Borrowdale and Trapney. The lab had made a note of the similar characteristics between them. There could be no doubt that they had been typed on the same machine.

27

Last Extracts from a Journal

▬ ▬ ▬ ▬ ▬ ▬ ▬ ▬ ▬ ▬ ▬ ▬ ▬ ▬ ▬ ▬ ▬

MONDAY

Bonnie. I can think about nothing else, write about nothing else. She has planted herself on me, this revolting pudding made in the shape of a woman. She says that we are together, that I must look after her. I have offered her the money from the magazine, not because I fear her but because she must *go away*. Take it, I said. She will not go. She wants us to go together, talks about assuming fresh identities, what she calls "starting up again." She wants to find more girls.

I reject her utterly. I despise her. She is the flesh, I am the spirit.

I reject her. But she is in *my* home, her snout is stuck into *my* books, she giggles and snuffles and shows her body to me, asking for what I shall not give her. She talks about the past, which I refuse to remember. I belong to the future.

This miserable swine snout has a revolver. Apparently she bought it through one of the boys in Dulwich, after a man came in and threatened her. That may be true. Anyway, she has a revolver and says she knows how to use it.

She sits in my room, filthy, sluttish, brooding on my books like a spider. I have taken this notebook away in case she sees it. She would give her meaningless fat laugh when she read it, would say it showed I was crazy.

She is under the impression that *she* is sane.

I can no longer tolerate her.

Comments and Reflections. The man who started to keep this notebook no longer exists. That man wrote letters signed Abel, which was the mask of Bela, he was Count Dracula and played always a game of masks. His life was all a pretense, but I have turned pretense into reality, I have experienced in my own body and soul what the Master called the transvaluation of All Values. When my troubles run deepest, and they are now very deep, I read his words and am comforted. I set down three quotations.

"Morality is a way of turning one's back on the will to existence."

"None of you has the courage to kill a man, or even to whip him."

"We resist the idea that all great human beings have been criminals (only in the grand and not in a miserable style), that crime belongs to greatness."

I take all these words for my own. Such words were my deeds. "Pain is something different from pleasure—I mean it is *not* its opposite," He said. Yet pleasure, and the will to power over others, is inextricably mixed with pain.

Because I say these things, and have fulfilled my words, should I be called mad? I can face the name.

He also became at last what the world calls mad. To Strindberg He signed himself Nietzsche Caesar, said that he had summoned a Council of Princes at Rome and would have the young Kaiser shot. He said that he had had Caiaphas put in chains, and had abolished Bismarck and all anti-Semites. Or He believed himself to be the Godhead and promised to arrange good weather. These dream imaginings were possible only to a man who had abandoned all worldly masks.

From this moment I abandon them too. The Game and the Players belong to the past. I have endured, have suffered, have achieved the Transvaluation of All Values, I am Friedrich Wilhelm Nietzsche. Everything else in my life was a pretense.

28

The Right Piece Falls into Place

━━ ━━ ━━ ━━ ━━ ━━ ━━ ━━ ━━ ━━ ━━ ━━ ━━ ━━ ━━ ━━

"Sergeant Plender I have met before, but a chief inspector," Mr. Borrowdale said. "Dear me. I take it that you want to see me about the unhappy affair at Planter's Place. Although what is unhappy for one may be happy for others. Do you know that I have sold the property? And that I had the pleasure of turning down two offers before accepting this one? Morbid curiosity is a wonderful thing. But how can I help you?"

He flexed his large hands, and his walnut-sized knuckles cracked. It struck Plender that he was uneasy, but he knew that many people are made uneasy by the presence of the police. Plender had spent a busy half hour on the telephone finding out something about the estate agent. He was a widower, was looked after by a housekeeper, and had been for some years a member of the town council. There was no longer a Trapney, and his business was not flourishing. The general opinion was that he needed a partner.

Hazleton had decided on a direct, although not impolite approach. "Mr. Borrowdale, I believe your firm uses or has used an Adler typewriter."

"Have we really? I didn't know that. I'll just ask Mrs. Stephenson." He began to get up. Plender rose at the same moment.

"I'll do it if you don't mind."

A middle-aged woman and a young girl sat in the outer office. The woman was using a Remington typewriter, the girl was doing filing. Plender closed the door of Borrowdale's office behind him. "Mrs. Stephenson? I wonder if you'd mind answering one or two questions."

Mrs. Stephenson had a bosom like a shelf, and a militant look. She said to the girl, "Rose, you can have half an hour off for shopping."

"How do you mean? I don't want any shopping."

"Go out, and don't come back for half an hour."

"But it's raining."

"Then go and stand in a doorway and watch the rain."

"Oh, I see. You don't want me here." She put on her coat and went out.

Mrs. Stephenson sighed. "Girls aren't what they used to be, and the change is for the worse. Now, Sergeant, if you are going to ask questions about Mr. Borrowdale's affairs, I should prefer him to be present."

"I've asked him this same question, and he referred me to you. It's very simple. Do you use an Adler typewriter, or have you had one in the past?"

"No."

Plender was taken aback. Mrs. Stephenson looked the incarnation of the president of every Mothers' Union. His surprise was obvious, and she took matronly pity on him.

"I have worked for ten years in this office, and I have never used any machine except that one."

He ran a hand through his hair. "There is another typewriter. Or there was. There must have been."

"Young man, are you calling me a liar?" The thought was terrible. "You may take my word for it that no other typewriter has been used here except this one. I call it Old Faithful."

He gulped, and then produced the particulars of Planter's Place. "Then where did this come from? It was issued by your firm, and typed on an Adler."

She looked at the sheet as though it were unclean. "That was not typed in this office. Of course the property has been sold now, but these are the details we sent out." She crossed to the girl's table, and brought back a sheet which she handed to him. The wording was almost identical, but the typewriter used was obviously a different one.

He ran a hand through his hair again. "Mr. Borrowdale himself gave me that one. It's got your letterhead at the top."

The great plateau of Mrs. Stephenson's bosom almost touched him. "So it has. But it was not typed here. I can only suggest that you ask him where it came from." With motherly amusement she said, "You might run a comb through your hair first. It's standing on end."

He returned to Borrowdale's office in a slightly dazed condition, and gave the two sheets to Hazleton. "Mrs. Stephenson says they've never had any typewriter but her Remington, which typed *this* one but not the other."

Hazleton tapped the one typed on the Adler. "You say Mr. Borrowdale gave you this one himself."

"That's right."

The DCI addressed Borrowdale. "Where did it come from?"

The estate agent flexed and cracked again. Then he grinned politely, showing yellow horse teeth. "Upon my word, I'm afraid I have no idea."

Hazleton's eyes popped dangerously. "You gave it to Sergeant Plender yourself."

"I did? Does it matter very much?"

"Yes, Mr. Borrowdale. Very much."

"It came from the cabinet behind you," Plender said. "Perhaps there are some more copies in there."

"I usually keep just one or two copies of particulars in here." He went to the cabinet. Plender stood behind him. "Yes, here we are. I gave you one, and here's another. That's the lot, I'm afraid."

Plender looked at it. "But this is typed on your own Remington."

"I've had enough of this, Mr. Borrowdale," Hazleton said. "I don't think you're being frank with us."

Borrowdale now looked very nervous indeed. "Oh dear. May I have Mrs. Stephenson in? I do rely on her a great deal, I'm afraid."

Hazleton nodded. Mrs. Stephenson entered the room, massive and imperturbable. Borrowdale's voice had a distinct quaver. "Mrs. Stephenson, these gentlemen want to know where these particulars came from, and I simply have no idea. Please do try to help."

She folded massive arms. "Not from this office."

Hazleton's voice rose slightly. "But it's your letter heading, woman, it was in your file."

"There is no need to shout." Plender was interested to see that her glance quelled the DCI. "Shouting will not help. This was not done while I was here." She put a hand to her chest. "My pneumonia."

Plender dared not look to see Hazleton's reaction.

"Two years ago I had pneumonia. It was just about that time we became joint agents for Planter's Place. These will be the old particulars."

Mr. Borrowdale tapped his bald forehead. "Foolish of me. Your pneumonia, of course, that's the answer."

The DCI's voice throbbed like an engine being kept forcibly under control. "I may be foolish myself, but I don't understand. What's the answer? Do you mean that another agent handled Planter's Place too?"

"Certainly. It's quite common. They had had the sole agency but hadn't sold it, so Mr. Medina decided to try us as well. It's customary to share the commission in the event of a sale."

Plender interrupted. "When I saw you before, you never told me that you were only joint agents."

Mr. Borrowdale stared at him, and then said simply, "You never asked me."

"So that this other agent would also have had keys, and access to Planter's Place."

"Certainly."

"I still don't see what Mrs. Stephenson's pneumonia had to do with it," Hazleton said.

"I was away, so we got a temp in, but she wasn't much good. The younger generation don't like work. So to save some typing, the existing sheet was just put in the copying machine and a few copies made under our letterhead. Later on, after I returned, I typed out the particulars properly. Mr. Borrowdale just happened to give you one of the old ones."

"So that the Adler typewriter belongs to the other firm, the joint agents. And who are they?"

Mr. Borrowdale's hands flexed, his knuckles cracked. "Darling's, in Bishopsgate."

Monday. Sixteen hundred hours. Alice Vane put down the telephone. Her mother hovered like a kite hawk.

"That was the police. They telephoned instead of coming because they weren't sure where to find me."

"He's been arrested." Mrs. Parkinson spoke as though she had been compelled to swallow some particularly nasty medicine.

"Paul has hanged himself. It seems the police wanted to talk to him, and he thought—I don't know what he thought. He was in Hampshire, taking a course of some kind."

"At least it was not at home." Alice looked hard at her mother. "I don't want to sound unsympathetic, but I can't be a hypocrite. It's a blessing in disguise. I always said he was no good."

"So you did, Mother. But do you have to say it again now?" She took a piece of paper and began to make notes. They ran: *Tell Jennifer. Tell office. Inquest? ask police.* Her mother was still standing there. "I shan't need any help."

She made her telephone calls, then went up to her room. She had brought away a photograph of Paul when she had first known him, eager, gay, to her eyes almost intolerably handsome. She turned over the frame. Then she began to cry. Outside, rain drove onto the windows.

Monday. Sixteen thirty hours. Bob Lowson had said the proper things to Alice, who sounded remarkably composed. Then he spent, as he afterward told Valerie, a bad ten minutes while he wondered whether Paul's death was in some degree his responsibility, whether he really had killed those girls, and whether the suicide would affect Timbals. After deciding that his conscience was clear and that serious repercussions were unlikely, he told Brian Hartford the news.

Brian was silent. Then he said, "I should like to see Esther Malendine get the job. Would you have any objection?"

For a moment Lowson was disconcerted by this reaction. Then he said, "I don't think so."

Hartford's even tones came down the office telephone. "I had nothing against Vane, you know. He thought I had, but he was wrong. He was just out of date in dealing with personnel problems, that was all."

These words, and Alice's quickly dried tears, were the nearest anybody got to an epitaph for Paul Vane.

Monday. Seventeen thirty hours. The adenoidal girl in Darling's office was operating a Royal typewriter, and knew nothing about an Adler. When she said that he had gone for the afternoon, Hazleton replied jovially that he was coming back after all, and had asked them to wait in his office.

There they found a good deal of correspondence about prospective sales of houses, but no safe, no locked drawers, and nothing relevant to the crimes until Plender, pulling out volumes of the *Estate Agent's Review* from a bookcase, noticed that two or three of them were free from dust. Behind them he found a book covered in limp blue leather, of the kind that was once used for standard editions of famous novelists. He looked at one or two pages, then passed it over to Hazleton.

Monday. Eighteen thirty hours. "Let's have some light," Paling said. The rain had stopped, but the threat of thunder hung in dark clouds outside. Brill turned on the light. Paling finished reading the blue book, put it down, sighed.

"The bugger's daft," Hazleton said. "Right round the bend."

"He impressed you as sane enough when you saw him."

"And who's this man he's on about, this Nitchie?"

"A German philosopher," Paling said loftily. He steepled his white fingers. "Odd, isn't it, how when the right piece falls into place—and here it was learning that Darling had at one time been joint agent for Planter's Place—everything becomes plain. Who is the man who knows where to get rid of a body, knows which houses are empty? An estate agent. And that explains the use of Vane's typewriter. Darling spotted it at Bay Trees and made use of it. Then, when he and Brown had killed the French girl, he buried her in the cellar."

Plender coughed, interrupted. "She wasn't killed at Bay Trees.

Hazleton moved restlessly. "We ought to be getting after him."

Paling smiled pleasantly. "Bear with me. This won't take five minutes, and it does have some point. Brown gets frightened, goes away, comes back, and Darling puts her in charge of his sex magazine. We don't know anything about that, except that he started it for money, and then used it for murder. She dyes her hair, tarts herself up, puts on a pair of spectacles with clear glass, and there's Alberta Norman. She's tasted blood now, and she wants more." His fingers touched the limp leather, lingered on it. "Did you notice how she becomes the dominant figure after being the minor one at first, so that he's in rebellion against her. Second murder, done in the empty house, Planter's Place, body left there."

There was a roll of thunder, distant. A fork of yellow light ran down the sky. Paling went on.

"Third murder, the Wilberforce girl. Body found in Batchsted Farm pond, yet she wasn't killed there. I can see you're impatient, Hazleton, but this is the point. The first and

208

third killings were done at some place where it wasn't convenient to bury the bodies. For some reason the second one took place elsewhere. If we could find the place where those two murders were done, I have the feeling that's where Alberta Norman is. And him too, for that matter. Any suggestions?" He smiled and looked around. He's a clever devil when it comes to theory, you can't deny it, Plender thought. "There are a lot of empty houses on Darling's books, I don't doubt. Perhaps we should make a list of them. He lives with his sister, so home, I presume, is out. What is it, Hazleton?"

"The barn. Outside the house there's a big barn. His sister's fairly deaf. She wouldn't hear what went on, no more would the neighbors."

Brill thought it was time he said something. "Supposing there was something doing at the house the night the Allbright girl was killed; he'd have to take her somewhere else."

Paling smiled and nodded, a teacher pleased with his pupil. "Precisely."

Hazleton was rubbing his chin. "He offered to show me that barn on Saturday night."

Paling laughed with genuine amusement. "That sounds just his line. I think if you'd said you'd like to see it he'd have made some excuse. Let's get to the barn."

Brill began to lay on the transport. Hazleton felt that he had stood a good deal of Paling's pontification. The DCS had conveniently forgotten that only a few hours ago he had gone off to arrest Vane. "What about Vane?"

"What about him?"

"Where does he fit in?"

"He doesn't. It was stupid to try to get rid of the body. Otherwise he was unlucky, that's all."

29

Bonnie, Dracula, Friedrich

━━ ━━ ━━ ━━ ━━ ━━ ━━ ━━ ━━ ━━ ━━ ━━ ━━ ━━ ━━ ━━

Wherever she looked the images were of blood. The rust-colored curtains looked like blood after it had dried, when she had put her tongue to it and found it merely salt. Many of the books around the wall seemed to be bound in blood, so that she had only to run her fingers over their redness and saliva came into her mouth. The blotting paper on the desk might have been soaked in blood; it was in the Turkey carpet on the floor, in lampshades and in the loose covers on the armchairs.

There was real blood in the room too. The wooden structure at one end of the room had blood on it, in spots or in long ribbons; there were spots of blood on the surrounding floor; crude daubs of genitals on the wall behind had been made with a finger dipped in blood. All the images were of blood, and all excited her. They were images like those of the time when Bonnie and Clyde had been caught in the double brick cabin at the Red Crown Cabin Camp. "They wouldn't give up till they died," Bonnie had written. She would not give up now. There was a time when things had not been like this, a time belonging to a different person. That person had read the Bible with belief and passion. There were stories in it that made her shiver with terror and delight, and other stories of people who had the intense purity of white. She remembered saying, when asked what she had wanted to be, "I want to be a white person."

People had laughed because they did not understand. She had ceased to be white, and become a gray person. Then Bonnie had met Dracula, Joan Brown had become Bert Norman. Now she was a red person and nobody laughed. This red person was shut up. Bonnie was shut up with Dracula as that other Bonnie had been with Clyde.

And like Clyde, Dracula was useless. Not only for sex, but in every way. He sat now in a chair at the desk looking through the diamond panes of the window at the unnaturally dark July day only occasionally illuminated by a streak of lightning, his head hunched into his narrow shoulders like a hibernating bird. She had been here three days now. He had brought over food and drink, he had arranged that she should go across to the house and wash after his sister had gone to bed, but he had hardly spoken to her otherwise, and what he did say sounded to her like gibberish. When Bonnie and Clyde were in trouble they just moved on, and she had expected that they would do just that. If Joan Brown could change into Bert Norman, Bert Norman could change too. As for him, he could easily become a different person. They had all the money they needed. But he did not answer her arguments, hardly seemed to hear them. He kept talking about somebody called Frederick, and about a change that was taking place in him. At first she had been rather in awe of his high-flown talk. She had been frightened also of what they had done, as she had been frightened as a girl after doing things to dogs and cats, but she was not frightened now. Now she felt only impatience and contempt in relation to him. Yet she knew that without him she was in some way incomplete, that she would be a gray woman again. That must not happen. "They wouldn't give up till they died"—she had quoted that line to him, but still he paid no attention.

So she talked at him, and screamed abuse, and took off her clothes and walked about in front of him, and then put them on again and tried to coax him into saying what they should do. She even threatened him with the shiny blue revolver that she kept under the cushion of the sofa where she slept, putting it to her head and then to his, saying *bang bang*, flopping on the carpet, kicking up her legs. He took no notice. On this dark day he had come back from the office, where she had worked for him after that first meeting at the film exhibition, bringing some sandwiches. She was hungry, and stuffed them down eagerly. When he left in the morning she had asked what they were going to do, and he said that when he came back he would decide. But since his return, more than an hour ago, he had sat and watched the day darken, heard the thunder sound, seen the rain fall, and had said nothing meaningful.

Now the thunder was passing over, but rain still fell out of a leaden sky. She went and stood beside him to look out.

"Keep away. You disgust me."

"And you disgust me." She went across to the door and turned on the light. "Don't you even want to talk about what we're going to do?"

"No."

"I'll clear off. I'll go on my own." She knew that she would never do it.

Now he did turn to look at her. He said in his usual quiet, prissy voice, "What you do is not of the slightest interest to me."

Through the rainy windows the lights of cars could be seen in the road. He sighed.

"What is it?"

"It is the beginning of my new life."

"It's the bloody police." She saw clearly that last ambush, the treacherous friend, Bonnie and Clyde shooting it out together to the end. Bonnie had reached for her gun when the lawmen shot her. "Come on, let's give it to them." She was holding the shiny revolver.

They were in two cars, Paling and Hazleton in the first, Brill and Plender in the other. The first car drove in, the second stopped at the gate as arranged.

"You've met Darling, and his sister too. You do the honors,"

Paling had said, and Hazleton had nodded his thanks. Now the DCS stepped out straight into a puddle, and swore. He had no taste for this kind of thing, but felt it obligatory to be here. They had tried to get hold of the chief constable, but happily he had not returned from a horse show.

Hazleton had been prepared for Isabel Darling to open the door, but not for the smile of welcome. "Inspector. You've come to look at my phlox. But I'm afraid you've chosen the wrong day and time for it. Do come in, and your friend too; you'll be soaked."

They had seen a light in the barn, but Plender and Brill were out there, and it was possible that Darling might be in the house. His sister sat them down in the tidy drawing room, sat down herself and smiled at them again.

"It's Jonathan you want to see, I know; that was only a little joke about the phlox. That tiresome case again, I suppose."

"That's right."

"He's in his study, and he doesn't like to be disturbed. Is there anything I can do?"

"His study? You mean the barn?"

"Yes. He likes to be alone there, you know. I never disturb him, not even to take over a cup of tea. It's his sanctum."

Hazleton was on his feet saying thank you, when Paling spoke. "There *is* just one thing you might help with, Miss Darling. The matter of a date. Do you by any chance keep a diary?"

He had to repeat the question. She blushed delicately. "How did you know, Superintendent—it is Superintendent, isn't it? I've kept one since I was fifteen. I remember, because the year I started it was tragic. Jonathan's brother Clayton was killed. He fell off a cliff, trying to help Jonathan up. My parents blamed Jonathan afterwards; for quite a long time they sent him to Coventry. I thought it was very unjust; I wrote reams about it."

"It was a date this year I wondered about. Monday, June the twentieth. I wondered whether anything particular happened that day."

"I can soon tell you." She went out of the room.

Hazleton stirred uneasily. It was like the Toff to say "You do the honors," and then take things over himself.

Plender and Brill had walked up the drive. They stood in the lee of the other car, looking at the barn. There was a light in it, but they could see nothing inside. They did not speak to each other, but just stood staring at the barn and getting wet.

She was across to the door and had turned the key in the lock, almost before he knew what she was doing.

"Give it to me."

She dropped the key down the neck of her sacklike dress. "You won't try to take it by force, I know that."

He stood motionless, looking at her. "Useless. You can't resist reality."

She waved the revolver. "We'll see about that. No stinking copper takes Bonnie, I can tell you."

The diary was covered in green velvet, and opened with a key which she took from a chain round her neck. As she turned the pages, Paling saw that they were filled with round feminine handwriting. He wondered what she found to write in it.

"Monday, June twentieth." She read what she had written, then looked up. "I'm afraid there's nothing to interest you. Jonathan's name isn't even mentioned."

"Perhaps he was out?"

"Oh yes, he was. You see, it was the Church Study Group night."

"The Church Study Group?"

"What did you say?"

Feeling like a fool, he repeated loudly, "The Church Study Group."

"That's right. We meet here always on the third Monday of

each month. For discussion and refreshment. Jonathan is always out. I am afraid he is not a believer."

Paling looked at Hazleton. This was the reason why Louise Allbright had not been brought to the barn. Isabel was deaf, but the other members of the Church Study Group were not. Theory had been justified. This time, when Hazleton rose Paling got up too. Isabel looked at them in surprise.

"We had a very good discussion about juvenile delinquency among those who attend church compared—"

"Thank you, Miss Darling," Hazleton said. "Now we'll talk to your brother in the barn."

They left her with her hands on the green velvet. How much did she know or suspect?

Outside, Hazleton resumed authority. The two sergeants, with two detective constables, were by the car.

"He's in that barn. The woman too, probably. Brill, come with me. Smith and Vesey, over by the gate in case there's another way out and he tries to use it. Plender, stay here."

It was twenty yards from the car to the barn. Hazleton and Brill had covered ten of them when one of the leaded windows opened. There was the sound of a shot, then two more. Brill cried out, dropped to the ground. Hazleton moved to one side, out of range of the window. Brill lay groaning. Before Paling could give an order, Plender ran forward, bent almost double, and began to half lift, half drag Brill to the safety of the car. Smith ran from the gate to help him. Paling beckoned to Hazleton to come back, and the DCI ran around beside the house to rejoin them. Two more shots were fired before they had Brill back behind the car.

"Got me in the leg." He grinned up at Plender. "Thanks, mate. Good job I'm not wearing my best suit, dragging me through the mud like that."

"Get him in the car." Hazleton ripped the trouser leg,

dabbed at blood with a handkerchief. "Flesh wound. You'll live." He turned back to Paling. "Question is, what do we do about chummy?"

They heard a voice from the barn, half shout, half shriek, another shot, then silence.

"I could go round, stay out of range and try the door," Plender suggested.

"I don't want anyone else hurt," Paling said. "The door may be locked."

"Six shots." Hazleton wiped water off his nose. "Reloading. Or could be just six shots."

They stood there for another minute. There was no sound from the barn. Paling could feel damp coming through what had been sold to him as a showerproof coat. Hazleton and Plender were looking at him. Some decision had to be made.

"All right. Hazleton, you, Smith and Vesey take the left side. Plender, you and I take the right. Meet by the door. If it's locked we charge it. If they start shooting, get back and take cover. Ten seconds." He drew out his watch. "Now."

Paling and Plender made good targets as they ran across to the right-hand side of the barn, but there was no firing. The other three were more under cover, and reached the barn door first. Hazleton turned the handle, pushed, then said, "Break it down."

They ran back half a dozen steps, charged. The door splintered, broke. They burst into the room, Paling and Plender just behind them.

The barn had been made into a comfortable study, carpeted, with a comfortable sofa and two armchairs, several bookshelves. Round the walls were pinned film stills. There was one showing a stake being driven through the heart of a vampire, and in others a man-headed bat bent over to bite a woman's throat, a dummy woman was being made into flesh, a woman in the grip of the Iron Maiden was being squeezed to death, a naked man hung upside down while another man prepared to cut out his

216

heart. In the midst of these stills was a large framed portrait of a man with a bushy mustache and a weak chin. None of the policemen recognized him as Friedrich Wilhelm Nietzsche.

But they did not look at these things. They stared, all of them, at one end of the room. There a roughly made wooden crucifix had been nailed to the wall. The white wood of which it was made was liberally stained with red. Above was a finger painting of male genitals done in the same red. Just at the foot of the crucifix was a stool.

"They tied them to it standing on the stool with a rope round the neck," Paling said. "When they'd had their fun they just took away the stool."

Plender bent over the body that lay near the foot of the crucifix. It was that of a dumpy woman with frizzy golden hair showing dark at the roots. There was a small hole at one side of her forehead, and just a little blood. The revolver was still clasped in one pudgy hand. Plender straightened up.

"Joan Brown."

Hazleton had already turned to the other end of the barn, and the rest of them turned with him. Little Mr. Darling had been sitting in one of the chairs, but now he got up and moved toward the policemen. His gray suit was uncreased, his blue tie discreet. He looked what he was, respectable. The smile on his lips was both nervous and wistful.

Hazleton coughed. "Jonathan Darling, I arrest you—"

Darling made a gesture in the direction of the portrait on the wall, then held up his hand. His voice, as always, had his own neat small tidiness. "My name is Nietzsche Caesar," he said. "I have effected in my own person the Transvaluation of All Values. I forgive you all."